When the Moon Is Full

WHEN THE MOON IS FULL

*Supernatural Stories from the
Old Pennsylvania Mountains*

BY ROBIN MOORE

Alfred A. Knopf
New York

THIS IS A BORZOI BOOK
PUBLISHED BY ALFRED A. KNOPF, INC.

Text copyright © 1994 by Robin Moore

Manufactured in the United States of America
1 3 5 7 9 10 8 6 4 2

Library of Congress Cataloging-in-Publication Data
Moore, Robin.
When the moon is full : supernatural stories from the old
Pennsylvania mountains / by Robin Moore.
p. cm.
Summary: A collection of tales of the supernatural based on the
traditional stories told in the mountains of Central Pennsylvania.
ISBN 0-679-85642-0 (trade)
1. Tales—Pennsylvania. 2. Horror tales. [1. Folklore—
Pennsylvania. 2. Horror stories.] I. Title
PZ8.1.M7797Wh 1994
[398.2'0974805]—dc20 94-13356

To Mim and Pop

Thanks for your help along the trail...

❧

A WELCOME,
A WORD OF WARNING...

WELCOME.

This is a collection of strange and supernatural stories from the mountains of central Pennsylvania.

Here you'll find the story of a wolf hunter enchanted by a woods witch, a boy who uses a bobcat skull to defeat an evil sorcerer, and a girl who watches a stuffed panther return to life in the moonlight.

As you read these tales you will enter a wild world of mystery and danger, lit by moonbeams and starlight, where truth hides in the shadows, where even ordinary things become otherworldly.

But first a warning. These stories are not natural. They are supernatural. All of them are eerie and some are downright scary. So before we begin, let me tell you an old storyteller's trick for preventing nightmares.

Tonight, before you get into bed, I want you to take off your shoes—you probably do that anyway, right?—I want you to take off your shoes and put them underneath the bed, with the toes facing in opposite directions. If you do that, none of the stories in this book will give you troublesome dreams.

I first heard stories like these when I was a boy growing up in the mountains of central Pennsylvania, where my family has lived for nearly two hundred years. Even then I loved the dark, wild feeling of these tales.

As an adult, I have done my best to keep the old tales alive and to create some original ones based on the tales I heard while I was growing up. As any storyteller must, I have remembered, reshaped, and reworked these stories to make them come alive on the printed page.

I hope their magic will charm you, as it has me.

These stories are at their best when they are read aloud on a cool, windy night when the moon is full and the house is dark and quiet.

So turn down the lights, gather your courage, and enjoy these supernatural stories from the Pennsylvania mountains.

CONTENTS

When the Moon Is Full

STUFFED PANTHER

When Old Man Jake Samson returned from the Civil War in the summer of 1864, he found the family farm in ruins. When he'd left four years earlier, the farm had been like a gleaming jewel: sixty acres of prime bottom land along Penns Creek, just north of the Seven Mountain ranges in central Pennsylvania.

But the hard winters, spring floods, and dry summers had taken their toll on the old place: the barn and outbuildings were in disrepair, the farmhouse itself was in shambles, and the fields, once lush with corn and wheat, were choked with weeds and bristle briers.

Old Man Samson's wife had died while he was away, leaving their only daughter, sixteen-year-old Sarah, to run the place alone. Sarah had done her best: she was a hard and steady worker.

Even so, it was all she could do to keep a small garden going, and to keep the cow milked and the chickens fed. Neighbors stopped by to help out now and then. But in those days there was only a scattering of farms in Penns Valley, with miles of rutty dirt roads and dangerous stream crossings in between. After her mother died, Sarah spent the seasons alone, working on the place, holding things together until her father returned.

Then one day late in August, Jake Samson did return. Sarah was out in the barnyard scattering hen feed near the chicken coop when she saw a cloud of dust on the old farm road. A moment later her father galloped up on a frisky gray stallion.

"Hello, daughter!" His voice rang out, filling the barnyard.

Sarah straightened and surveyed her father. He looked much older than she remembered. His long chin whiskers had gone completely gray. But there was a twinkle in his eye as he swung down from the saddle and stepped through the barnyard gate. He was wearing the tattered remains of his blue Union uniform. His boots were scuffed and worn. On his right hip he carried his revolver in a black leather holster.

Then Sarah saw it—his left shirt sleeve hung empty, flapping in the wind as he came toward her.

She stepped back in horror. "Papa, your arm!"

The old man grinned. "Now, don't you worry 'bout that, Sarah. Give a hug for your old dad."

When Sarah hesitated, the old man said, "It's all right. You won't hurt me. I'm all healed up now."

Sarah stepped forward and put her arms around her father. It was awkward hugging a one-armed man, but she managed somehow, saying, "Welcome home, Papa." They embraced for a long moment there in the barnyard.

"They had to take the arm off," the old man explained. "I got my shoulder joint smashed by a musket ball at Chancellorsville. Where's your ma?"

Sarah stepped back and wiped her hands on her apron. "I guess you didn't get my letter."

The old man's face fell. "She's gone?"

Sarah nodded. "Died of cholera last spring. She went fast and asked for you till the end."

The old man leaned against a fence rail and ran his hand over his bald head.

"Poor Betsy. She never did like the farm life. Always wanted to live in town," he said sadly.

The old man raised his eyes and glanced at the barn. He saw the missing boards and the collapsing roof. Then his gaze slipped behind the barn to the fallen outbuildings, the fences that needed mending, and finally to the ruined fields beyond.

"I know the place looks bad," Sarah said quietly, "but we'll put things right, won't we, Papa?"

The old man stared for a long time, saying nothing. Then slowly the twinkle came back into his eye.

"Yes, we will, daughter, you and me. We'll put things right. You can't keep a good man down. That's what I always say."

Old Man Samson was right. You can't keep a good man down.

That fall the little farm along Penns Creek was a whirlwind of activity. Even one-armed, the old man was able to ply his carpentry skills. He resided the old barn and repaired the corncrib and the storage sheds. He and Sarah put a new roof on the woodshed and filled it with split stove wood for the winter.

With the food they had stored from the garden, with the cow, the chickens, a few wild deer and rabbits taken from the mountainside, and with a little luck, they would make it through the winter just fine.

Then, in spring, they would get out the old plow, hitch up the horse, and furrow the neglected fields into straight, dark rows. By summer the fields would be green and growing again.

They passed the summer there on the old place, putting things back together. And it seemed to Sarah that with each board nailed and each field reclaimed, her father was restored as well.

In the morning she could hear him singing out in the barn as he did his chores. At night she would sit out on the back porch in the glow of their kerosene lantern, listening as Old Man Samson told her about the early days on the farm, how he and Sarah's mother had worked side by side to wrest a living from the soil. How they had planted apple trees and grapes. How young Jake Samson had loved the woods and the fields. And how Betsy was a churchgoer and a socialite who loved picnics and dances and parties. Sometimes, the old man said, they would dress in their Sunday best and take the wagon into Roopsburg just to walk around and be seen together.

It seemed that telling about the early days revital-ized the old man. Through his words, Sarah strained her imagination, reaching back across the years, trying to grasp what it must have been like for her parents when they were young and in love, the juices of life roaring through their veins.

Then one cool October night something happened that changed Sarah's life forever. It was a strange night: blustery and cold, with the wind rattling the fence slats and shuddering through the trees.

The full moon looked especially strange. Sarah was getting ready for bed when she noticed it. She peered through the white curtains of her bedroom window, up on the second floor of the farmhouse, her face near the cold glass. The wind swept over and around the house, rattling the panes.

Sarah could see long purplish-gray clouds blowing across the face of the moon, making weird shapes. It was eerie, something her mother might have called an omen. But that was foolishness, Sarah thought. She was seeing nothing but wind and clouds and moonlight—nothing to make a fuss about. Sarah put on her white ankle-length nightdress and slipped into bed, under her heavy turkey-down quilt. Still, she couldn't sleep.

There was something about the sound of the wind—or maybe it was a sound mixed with the wind. Just then her father appeared in the dim light at Sarah's doorway, wearing his boots and his white long johns with one sleeve dangling. In his right hand he held his revolver.

"Sarah! There's something breakin' into the chicken coop! I'll need a light to shoot by."

Sarah leaped out of bed and pulled on her boots.

"I'll get the lantern, Papa."

"I'll meet you down there."

Sarah ran down the back steps to the kitchen. On the table was their heavy kerosene lantern. With shaking hands, Sarah raised the glass chimney, lit the wick with a big sulfur match, and settled the glass back into place.

As Sarah approached the barnyard, she saw her father crouched on the ground a dozen yards in front of the henhouse. His pistol barrel was trained on a large hole that had been ripped through the wooden slats on the side of the coop.

Sarah knew that every now and then a fox or a weasel would steal into the coop and go after the hens. But from the size of the hole and from the sound of the struggle inside, Sarah knew that they were dealing with something more dangerous than a fox or a weasel.

"Stay behind me with that light," her father said sharply. "If I got light in my eyes, I can't see. And if I can't see, I can't shoot."

Sarah held the lantern high.

She focused her eyes on the ragged hole.

"Hold steady," she heard her father say. "Whatever it is, it's comin' out."

A second later a huge mountain lion, the body of a

freshly killed chicken dangling from its mouth, stepped out into the lantern light. The wind came up, blowing leaves around the barnyard. For a long moment, that he-panther froze in the yellow lantern light, streams of breath issuing from its nostrils, blood dripping from its snout and whiskers.

Sarah and the panther stared at each other. There was something wild and fascinating in the animal's gaze. And for a moment she felt as if she were being hypnotized by those glowing yellow eyes.

Then she heard the sharp crack of her father's pistol a few feet off to her left. The big cat fell backward and collapsed against the wall of the chicken coop.

The old man rose, walked a few steps closer, and put another shot into the mountain lion's forehead. He walked even closer and poked at the hind legs with the barrel of his pistol. Then he straightened and turned into the lantern light.

"It's all right, daughter. He's dead now."

Still holding the lantern, Sarah slowly walked forward.

She had never seen a mountain lion up close before. Of course, she had often heard their screams up on the mountainside at night. And a few times she had seen panther tracks in the mud by the pond. But she had no idea that the cats got to be so big.

Old Man Samson used his pistol as a measure and calculated that the mountain lion measured nine feet from the tip of its nose to the tip of its tail.

He was long and lean and tawny, and sharp-clawed. Sarah couldn't resist reaching out to touch the luxuriant hair along his flanks.

She set the lantern on the ground beside the great beast and began stroking his honey-colored coat. Then her gaze went to his eyes. They were sad and vacant, staring at nothing. The wonderful hypnotizing light she had seen was gone.

For a moment Sarah was sorry the panther was dead. But, she told herself, that was silly. Her father had been right to shoot the big cat. You can't have wild animals coming down out of the woods and having their way with your chickens.

"Wait'll the boys see this one," the old man said proudly. "This is a real old-time mountain lion. People used to call 'em by different names. Some folks called 'em painters or panthers. Some called 'em pumas or catamounts or deer tigers. There used to be so many of 'em, we'd kill 'em on sight. We thought we'd never rid the mountains of 'em. But now there aren't that many left. I'll bet this is one of the last."

Sarah stroked the tawny fur, a strange feeling of sadness settling over her.

"Say," the old man said, "I want something to remember this night by. I'm gonna drag this big fella into the barn, skin him out in the morning, and make us a rug for the front room. That'll be downright impressive."

Leaving the body of the panther, Sarah knelt and

shined her light inside the chicken coop. It was a mass of blood and feathers. Not a single hen remained alive.

"I'm going off to bed, Papa. I'll clean this up in the morning."

The old man nodded. "You go ahead, daughter." Then he bent and began dragging the body of the panther up to the barn door.

To save kerosene, Sarah raised the chimney on the lantern and let the wind blow the flame out. As she walked back across the road and up to the farmhouse, she was aware of the strange moonlight again. Tilting her head back, Sarah watched as the wind swirled purplish clouds across the white face of the moon. It seemed as if the clouds had taken on the shapes of long-tailed panthers leaping across the moon.

"It's a panther moon tonight," she said to herself. She had once heard her mother use that phrase, and until now she had never understood what it meant. But it did seem, as she glanced overhead, that the clouds had formed themselves into the shapes of leaping and running panthers, speeding across the disk of the moon. But this was nothing more than an illusion created by exhaustion and commotion, Sarah assured herself. Her mind had become overexcited and made her see things that weren't really there. Sarah knew it would all seem silly in the light of day.

Back in her room, she pulled off her boots and slipped under the covers. But she couldn't sleep. She lay awake for the longest time, haunted by the sight of those glowing yellow eyes.

The next morning Sarah let herself sleep late. At last she rose and brushed out her hair, tying it back with a black ribbon. She put on her dress, a clean apron, and her work boots and headed downstairs. She had heard her father get up at dawn, and she knew he would be out doing the chores. He would appreciate a good breakfast when he got back.

Still sleepy, Sarah opened the door of the cast-iron stove, threw in a few sticks of kindling, and widened the draft to light the morning fire. But as she was straightening up, Sarah caught a strange shape out of the corner of her eye. Startled, she turned.

There, staring in the kitchen window at her, was that mountain lion.

"No," she said softly. "It can't be."

Just then her father came in the back door, chuckling to himself. When he saw the astonished look on Sarah's face, he burst out laughing.

"Papa, what's the meaning of this?"

"Here, I'll show you." He took Sarah by the hand and led her out the door onto the back porch. Sure enough, there was that mountain lion, standing like a statue on the porch, gazing into the window. For a moment Sarah thought the panther had somehow come back to life. Then she realized that he wasn't alive at all. He was stuffed, like the wild animals she had once seen in a museum in Philadelphia.

"I got up early," her father explained. "I was determined to skin out that panther and make us a rug. It took me a solid hour to get the skin off him. I did a real careful job, if I do say so myself. Then, as I was scraping down the skin, I got an even better idea. I decided I would make us something better than a rug."

Here her father broke into a fit of wild laughter and slapped his leg as if he were enjoying a joke that no one else knew. At last he composed himself enough to go on.

"I went into the back of the barn and I got some stiff fence wire and I crooked it up into the right shape. Then I laid that skin over it, stuffed it full of straw, and sewed up the legs and belly. Looks like a regular taxidermy job, wouldn't you say?"

Well, it did look like a regular taxidermy job, except for one thing. If Old Man Samson had been a taxidermist, he would have put glass eyes in the eyeholes. But he didn't have any. So he left them empty.

That was the strangest thing about it, to see that mountain lion standing there, lifelike as could be, with no eyes in the eyeholes, just a little bit of straw poking out.

Sarah was horrified. She rarely disagreed with her father, but this time she was firm.

"You're not bringing that thing in the house," she said.

"I don't intend to, daughter," the old man said good-naturedly. "I don't intend to."

"Well, then what are you going to do with it?"

Samson laughed. "You just watch."

The old man went into the barn and emerged a few moments later carrying the long wooden ladder they had used to roof the woodshed. He set the ladder against the long, sloping roof of the shed. Then he disappeared back into the barn and came out with a long hank of rope and a cloth sack of tools.

Chuckling to himself, Samson tied the rope around the mountain lion's torso. Holding one end of the rope, he climbed the ladder to the roof, then drew the lightweight body of the beast up behind him.

As Sarah watched in horror, the old man positioned the carcass on the ridge of the woodshed roof. With a heavy hammer he drove a long barn spike through each one of the panther's paws, nailing them to the roof of the shed. Then he bent the wire inside the tail so it crooked up, looking long and dangerous. He bent the forelegs, placing the panther in a crouching position, as if it were going to leap off the roof of the woodshed. Then, like the biblical Samson, he pulled open the jaws as wide as he could, exposing the panther's sharp teeth.

Samson climbed down and looked proudly at his handiwork.

Sarah walked up behind him, unable to take her eyes off the terrible thing.

"Papa, I don't like it. Take it down. It's just not right."

"Now you hush up. I declare, Sarah, you're becoming like your mother, always wanting to drain all the wildness and fun out of life. That thing's going to be a wonder."

And it was. The woodshed was just a few feet off the main road to Roopsburg, so every horseback rider and wagoner, every farmer, millwright, and housewife, and every child walking to school down that road would look up and see the panther crouched on the edge of the woodshed roof as if it were going to pounce on them.

And people loved that thing. They loved it and got a thrill out of seeing it. Many young people had never seen a real Pennsylvania mountain lion before. So the old-timers from all the surrounding farms brought their children to look and gawk and gossip. Sarah's father would walk them over to the chicken coop and show them the hole and repeat the story again and again about how he had dropped the panther with one shot from his revolver—a clean neck shot at twelve yards by lantern light. Everyone agreed that that was some shooting.

Sarah came to hate the gawkers and the loafers who congregated at the farm. They brought whiskey and bad manners and too much noise. Sometimes farm boys would sneak up in the dark of the night and chuck rocks at the panther, and once a few rowdies drove by in a wagon and took potshots at it with their shotguns. Of course, the bullets passed right through, leaving small holes in the panther's sides. Sometimes a little yellow straw spilled out of the bullet holes and was carried away by the wind.

Sarah pleaded with her father to be sensible and take the thing down, but he wouldn't hear of it.

"This is the most enjoyment I've had since I left for the war," the old man would say. "What was the point of fighting for the Union all those years if I can't have a little fun now and then?"

It *was* great fun, most everyone agreed. At least until the screams started.

Now, I don't know if you know—a mountain lion will mate for life. In the winter mating season, a she-panther, the mate of the male, came down off the mountainside and into the valley.

It's a strange call the female has: a scream that sounds almost human. Some old-timers describe it as a cross between a woman's scream and a howling winter wind. But there's something else in it, something wild and eerie, that raises the hairs on the back of your neck when you hear it. It's the sound of something that slips between the shadows and hunts in the night.

Having the panther so close to their farm animals made people nervous. It made the farm dogs nervous too. And every night when that female started screaming for her mate, the dogs in the valley would just go crazy, howling and yapping and barking until morning. After a week or so, the people in the valley got together and asked one of the preachers to go over and talk to Samson.

"Brother Samson," the preacher said, "if you don't take that thing down, the people in this valley will never get any sleep. They might as well cut their beds up for firewood."

"Oh, no," the old man said. "That mountain lion's gonna stay right there. Some night that she-panther's gonna get bold. She's gonna show herself. And I'm going to be right there with my pistol. Then I'll have two stuffed panthers up on my woodshed!"

But the she-panther didn't show herself. She always stayed back in the trees, just beyond Old Man Samson's fields.

There is one thing I forgot to tell you. You see, Sarah's bedroom window was just about level with the roof of the woodshed. Every night she would stand there, peering through her bedroom window curtains at the panther, crouched, nailed to the roof of the shed.

Sometimes at night, when the moon was shining full and bright, it seemed to Sarah that a strange kind of yellowish light would come into the panther's eyes. But then she realized: It was nothing but the moonlight glinting off the light-colored straw in the creature's eyeholes.

And sometimes when the wind would blow through the mountain lion's coat, it almost seemed to Sarah that he was moving, coming to life, straining against those

[17]

barn spikes, trying to get loose and follow his mate up into the hills where he belonged. But then she'd tell herself it was just a trick of the wind.

Then one night as Sarah was watching through her bedroom window curtains, the panther very slowly turned his head and looked at her with his shining yellow eyes. There was something in his look, something sad and haunting, a request that Sarah couldn't brush aside.

She knew what she had to do. And one evening deep in February, when her father had left for town and said he wouldn't be back until late, Sarah decided she would do what she could to turn the stuffed panther loose.

Sarah dressed warmly, lit her lantern, and went out into the windy, snowy night. It was a panther moon, all right: the purplish clouds leaped across the lunar disk, sped on by the wind. Sarah trudged out to the barn and went into her father's toolbox and found his heavy iron crowbar. She would pry those barn spikes loose. Then she would drag that stuffed panther out into the woods and pray that the she-panther would find him and that would be the last she would ever see of them.

She wouldn't need the ladder to climb up onto the roof. Her father had brought in a huge load of firewood and piled it against the shed, right up to the eaves. Sarah could just scramble right onto the log pile and crawl up the sloping roof to the ridge. She would work her way across, being careful of the wind and snow, and pry the panther loose.

The screams started just as she was closing the barn door and walking toward the shed. Then the dogs started barking.

Old Man Samson had just bought six new hunting dogs that week. He had them tied up on the back porch. Each night the she-panther's screams worked the dogs into a fury.

That night was no exception. But now the terrifying sound was shriller and more insistent than before. The dogs went crazy. They gnawed through their ropes and began racing around and around the woodshed, barking for all they were worth.

Then as Sarah watched in horror, one big hound scrambled up the log pile and leaped onto the roof of the shed. The other dogs crawled up behind him. Sarah shouted at them to get down. But her voice was carried away by the wind.

As she stood in the deep snow holding the crowbar, the dogs scratched their way up the steep woodshed roof and began to tear the stuffed panther to pieces.

Yellow light flashed from the panther's eyes as he twisted his neck, lunging out at the dogs. But he couldn't defend himself. His sharp-clawed paws were nailed firm to the roof of the shed. The snarling dogs closed in on him, tearing great rips in his flanks and shoulders. Shouting in fury, Sarah made her way through the deep snow and began to climb up the woodpile after the dogs.

Then out of the corner of her eye Sarah saw something move. It started back in the trees, a long, powerful form, moving fast across the snow. Sarah narrowed her eyes in the moonlight, trying to make out the shape. And then she knew. It was the she-panther!

That female came straight for the shed at a full run. In a single graceful leap she left the ground and landed on the roof of the shed, scrambling up to a fighting position beside her mate.

Taking the hounds by surprise, the tawny cat plunged in among them, slashing with her claws and tearing with her teeth. The dogs yelped in pain. Torn and bleeding, they tumbled down the roof of the shed and ran off behind the barn, trailing blood on the snow.

Sarah clung to the edge of the woodpile and watched in amazement as the she-panther turned to her mate and affectionately licked the bullet holes in his neck and forehead and at his side. The female looked down and saw the barn spikes and understood why her mate hadn't responded to her cries all those nights.

Then that pantheress did an amazing thing. Just as she'd do with one of her kittens, she bent down and used her teeth to take hold of the loose skin around the panther's right front paw. With a powerful motion, she tore his paw loose from the barn spike. The panther roared in pain as she yanked each of his paws loose.

And then without so much as a backward glance, the two panthers leaped off the woodshed and headed for the woods. But the male was weak and wounded. Halfway across the field he stumbled and fell. The female looped around and came back to stand beside him. By this time the dogs were getting bold again and had come around from behind the barn. They were barking and building up their courage to give chase.

The female nudged her mate with her snout to try to get him to rise and follow her. But he couldn't. Then, just as she'd do with one of her kittens, she grabbed hold of the loose skin around the male's neck, and straining every muscle, she dragged him across the moonlit field and into the shadow of the trees.

The dogs never did get the courage to chase the pair. Instead they just slunk back to their hiding place behind the barn.

Without knowing exactly why, Sarah followed the panthers a ways, out of the field and up into the trees on the mountainside. It was easy to spot their trail, even in the dark woods. In the places where the moonlight broke through the trees, Sarah could see handfuls of light-colored straw that glowed in the eerie light.

Sarah knelt and took a handful in her palm, knowing that these strands had spilled from the holes torn in the panther's side by the dogs. At last, when she was satisfied that the pair had gotten away, she rose and walked through the windy dark back to the farmhouse and put herself to bed.

When Old Man Samson returned late that night, he noticed that the stuffed panther was gone. Nothing remained of his trophy but four well-placed barn spikes sticking up through the shingles on the roof of the woodshed. Glancing down, he saw the tracks of his dogs. The snow was stained with blood that looked black in the moonlight.

Following the trail, Samson located the wounded, lacerated dogs behind the barn. He realized they were ruined for hunting. Reluctantly, he pulled his pistol and put them out of their misery.

Sarah started awake at the sound of shots. She rose, lit the lantern, and went down to the kitchen. She knew her father would want a cup of coffee. She wasn't sure how much she should tell him. She was glad to see the stuffed panther freed and wanted it to stay that way. She was afraid that given half a chance, the old man would hunt those panthers down so he could erect both grisly carcasses on the roof of the woodshed.

Just then he came through the kitchen door and asked, "Sarah, what's happened here?"

She shook her head. "Papa, it was dark and I was scared. I couldn't tell for sure what happened. I think those dogs must have fought one another over that stuffed panther, and they must have torn it to pieces."

The old man nodded. "That stuffed panther was fun for a while. But now it's cost me six fine dogs. I'll tell ya, daughter, I'm glad to be rid of the danged thing."

And that was the last she ever said to her father about the panther and its mate.

Long after, Sarah wondered about them. She wondered if the male had healed and if the she-panther had been able to bring him back to life somehow.

Then one night she got her answer. That spring, Sarah and Stephen Yuengling, a fine young man from one of the neighboring farms, started to take an interest in each other. Stephen often came over courting in the evenings, after the work was done. On moonlit nights they loved to walk away from the house, down to a small pond by the mountainside.

One full-moon night they were walking—walking and talking as young lovers do—when Sarah noticed two strange shapes on the opposite side of the pond. At first she thought they were logs lying in the water. But as she looked more closely she could see that they weren't logs at all. They were the long, lean bodies of two panthers crouched and drinking at the pond.

Stephen reached for his pistol, but Sarah placed a hand on his.

"No," she said quietly, "they won't harm us. I know them."

The panthers continued drinking, lapping up the water with their long tongues as Sarah and Stephen watched, amazed.

Then the smaller of the two, the female, raised her head and looked across the pond at them. Sarah looked into the she-panther's glowing yellow eyes. The larger of the two, the male, raised his head, and Sarah took her breath in sharply. He didn't have any eyes in the eyeholes, just a little bit of straw poking out.

The four lovers stood there a long time, across the water from one another. Then the female nudged her mate with her snout and the two turned and ran, shoulder to shoulder, off into the woods.

❦

YEARS LATER, after her father had died and she and her husband were raising their own children on the family farm, Sarah told Stephen everything about the stuffed panther. He never questioned the truth of the story, because he had seen the eyeless panther himself.

As Sarah's children were growing up, she often took them for walks at night, down to the pond and around the fields. This was long after the last of the big cats had disappeared from the Pennsylvania mountains.

But sometimes at night Sarah's children would lift their faces to the sky, watching the purplish clouds glide across the surface of the moon, and they would say, "Mama, it's a panther moon tonight, isn't it?"

And Sarah would smile in the darkness.

"Yes," she would say, "it is."

SKULLPLAYER

One day while picking berries in a low and swampy meadow, a small boy found the skeleton of a bobcat. The flesh and hair had long since fallen from the bones and been washed away into the swampy ground, leaving behind a delicate whitened cluster of bones, stacked like crockery in the deep moss.

The boy was fascinated and examined the skeleton with great care. Everything was there: the curved rib bones, the graceful string of backbones, the catlike legs and shoulder blades. But it was the bobcat's skull that interested him most. It was polished and rounded and surprisingly heavy for its size. Hefting it, the boy found that it fit easily into the palm of his hand. There was something else: Even though the lower jaw had fallen away, the sharp upper teeth still projected from the front of the skull. This was a marvel.

The boy began tossing the skull into the air and catching it. Perfect balance. Soon the boy was running through the meadow, rolling the skull, kicking it, and throwing it like a ball. Then he discovered something more: Whenever he threw the skull up against an old tree or a dead stump, the sharp front teeth would bite and stick in.

The boy took the skull home with him. In the days that followed, he spent hours playing with his new toy. He soon became very skillful at rolling and throwing it. He could strike any target with those pointed teeth. He made a deerskin shoulder bag to carry the skull in, and from that day forward he was never seen without it.

The people in the boy's village marveled over the skull as well. And because of his skill with it, the people called him Skullplayer.

Skullplayer was the youngest of four Lenape Indian brothers. The Lenape lived in the river valleys of what is now called Pennsylvania. Of course, this was long before William Penn or any other Europeans had come to this land.

This was in the days when the mountains of central Pennsylvania were misty and quiet, a lonely place for humans but home to thousands of animals—deer, timber wolves, elk, black bear, woods bison, wild turkey, beaver, toads, blacksnakes, otter, weasels.

Each fall it was the custom of the four brothers to leave their village in the lowlands and head up into the mountains. There they would set up a hunting camp and hunt all through the fall into early winter. When they had dried enough meat and collected enough pelts and deerskins for the winter, they would return to their village and spend the rest of the season in comfort, listening to the old people's stories by the fire.

One autumn when Skullplayer was eight years old, he and his three brothers, Cornstalk, Blue Hawk, and Slow Turtle, set up a hunting camp in a boggy place that is now called Black Moshannon. The deer hunting was exceptionally good there, and it had plenty of rabbit holes and beaver ponds.

This was how they would pass their days. The brothers would rise before dawn and hunt for several hours in the morning light. They would return to camp in the afternoon to dry their meat and scrape their pelts. Then they would venture out again just before sunset. Sometimes they hunted at night by torchlight.

Of course, Skullplayer never hunted. He was too young. And besides, he had never shown any interest in bows or arrows. He was too busy playing with his bobcat skull. So he stayed behind in camp, sometimes guarding the meat racks from crows and doing the small camp chores. At night Skullplayer would tell his brothers ridiculous, unbelievable stories about animals he had met in the forest. The four brothers enjoyed themselves in this way all through the early days of fall.

Then one morning a strange thing happened. Skullplayer's oldest brother, Cornstalk, was walking through the woods hunting deer, when he came upon a large beaver pond. He hid behind a cluster of birch trees and waited, hoping to catch a glimpse of a beaver. After a short time he saw a dark shape moving through the water, something black and sleek and graceful. But it wasn't a beaver. When he looked more closely, he could see that it was a beautiful young woman swimming through the water with her long black hair trailing behind her.

As Cornstalk watched in amazement, she pulled herself up on a log and began to comb out her hair with an elk antler comb. The young man's eyes drank in her beauty. Water streamed from her hair and off the simple lines of her buckskin dress, down to her delicate bare feet.

Cornstalk was so captivated by her beauty that he instantly wanted her for his wife. So he did what young Lenape men usually did when they were struck with the lovesickness. He reached into his quiver and pulled out his love flute. Made from cedar wood, love flutes are about as long as a man's forearm and are played by blowing into the end of the flute and fingering the note holes.

Cornstalk raised the flute to his lips and blew a sad and beautiful tune out across the misty water. As soon as the liquid notes reached her, the woman stopped combing and glanced into the trees where Cornstalk was hiding. Then she smiled a radiant smile, like sunlight glinting off the water. Cornstalk stopped playing. He wanted to stand up and walk down to the water's edge, revealing himself to her. But he couldn't. Like many young men at moments like this, he was overcome with shyness.

Then, suddenly, in one graceful motion, she tucked her comb into her belt and slipped into the water, disappearing beneath the surface. Furious at himself for his lack of courage, Cornstalk ran down to the edge of the pond and peered into the murky waters, hoping to catch some glimpse of her. But she was gone.

Walking back to camp that afternoon, Cornstalk wondered if it had really happened. Maybe what he had seen was a dream woman. He considered telling his brothers, but something prevented him from mentioning it. Perhaps he was afraid they would laugh at him. After all, he was the oldest and should act responsibly. He shouldn't spend their hunting season dreaming of young women.

But early the next morning he found himself crouched behind the birches with his flute tucked into his belt and his eyes fixed on the placid surface of the beaver pond. As the first rays of morning light were striking the water, Cornstalk thought he saw a movement in the center of the pond. And suddenly there she was, swimming easily to the surface, her hair like a sleek black waterfall as she pulled herself up on the log and began combing out her hair.

Cornstalk was so overwhelmed by her beauty that he almost forgot to play the flute. But then, as her sparkling black eyes glanced up in his direction, he remembered. He played a long, lavish love song of liquid notes, a song he hadn't known before. As the last note faded away, so did she. She slipped into the water and was gone, leaving behind a slight ripple to mark where she had been.

Cornstalk dashed down to the water, trying to comprehend what had happened. For a single mad moment he considered throwing off his deerskin shirt and leggings and diving into the water after her. But he was afraid. The waters of the pond were green and murky, and he was a poor swimmer. He turned quietly and went back to camp.

It went on like that for four lovesick days. Each morning Cornstalk would play his flute and each morning the young woman would smile and swim away, as mysterious as ever. But still he couldn't summon the courage to show himself to her.

Of course the three brothers knew something was going on. It was clear that Cornstalk had lost any interest in hunting. He seemed to spend his days in solitary walks. At night he was moody and silent by the fire.

At last it was Skullplayer who spoke up.

"I have heard your flute during the mornings, somewhere off to the south of camp. Whom are you playing to?" he asked.

But before Cornstalk could answer, a voice on the edge of the fire ring said, "He plays to me."

And a beautiful woman came walking up into the firelight. She moved with the grace of someone who knows exactly where she is going. The brothers sprang to their feet in amazement. She walked straight up to the oldest brother and took his face in her hands.

"I am Waterwoman," she said in a voice that sounded like rippling waters. "I have heard your love song out across the water. And I want to be your wife. But before you answer I must warn you. The man who marries me and the family who takes me in will be in great danger. When I was a small girl, I was stolen from my family by Old One Eye, the evil sorcerer who lives far back in the swamps. He steals young women away from their families and keeps them as his slaves for as long as he likes. When he grows tired of them, he feeds them to the Ya-Kwa-Hey, his fierce hairless bear.

"I was his captive for years. But I paid attention. I learned something of his chants and incantations. I tricked him into changing me into a waterwoman, a woman who can live underwater. And I have lived in that pond ever since. But the other morning, when I heard the sound of your cedar flute, I remembered how good it was to live on the land, among people. I want to become part of your family. I want to become a land-woman again."

Cornstalk said yes. What else could he say? He was stricken with love for her. His brothers agreed they would do everything they could to protect the young woman, and they lived together happily for some time. The three older brothers went hunting every day, and Waterwoman stayed back in camp, drying the meat and preparing their meals. Skullplayer stayed behind too, but now he had an important job: He had been instructed to keep an eye out for the old sorcerer. If he saw anyone approaching who looked suspicious, he would warn

Waterwoman so she could make a dash for the pond, where she would be safe.

But you know how Skullplayer was. As much as he admired Waterwoman, he sometimes wished he were free, as he had been before, to roam the woods and play with his bobcat skull So one afternoon while Waterwoman was busy scraping deer hides, Skullplayer slipped away and spent the whole day in the woods, rolling his skull and enjoying himself.

When he came back to camp late in the afternoon, he was horrified by what he saw. Waterwoman's cooking implements were scattered around. The wooden meat rack had been knocked down, and by the signs on the ground in the center of camp, he could see that there had been a huge struggle. He knew that Old One Eye had come back and stolen Waterwoman away.

You see, Old One Eye knew everything that was happening in their camp. He knew everything that went on between Waterwoman and the brothers without ever leaving his bark-covered lodge in the deep of the swamp. His messengers, the black crows who sometimes stole meat from the drying racks, brought him the news every day.

Skullplayer knew he had failed. When his brothers returned, he told them everything and ended by saying, "I am no longer worthy of your trust."

Cornstalk laid a hand on his younger brother's shoulder. "Don't blame yourself. I am the one who has failed. Waterwoman is my wife. I was the one who should have guarded her. And now I am the one who must go and get her back."

Cornstalk went into their bark hut and began to dress himself for war. He blackened his face with soot and tied back his hair. He stuck his war club in his belt and shouldered his bow and a quiverful of arrows.

"Before I go, I want to show you boys something." Cornstalk reached into his quiver and drew out his love flute.

"There is great magic in this flute. Skullplayer, I want you to keep this. If I don't return by tomorrow morning, play a love song on the flute. If a single droplet of blood falls from its end, you will know that I am dead. You must pack your things and move from this place. Go back to the village where you will be safe."

His brothers protested, but Cornstalk wouldn't listen to them. "If you love me as your brother, you will not endanger yourselves." Then he laid his flute on a log by the fire and set off for the sorcerer's camp.

Their trail was easy to find. Old One Eye had carried Waterwoman away with her arms dangling down over his back. She had managed to grab on to bushes and branches, snapping them off and dropping them, leaving a trail Cornstalk could easily follow. Cornstalk plunged deeper and deeper into the swamp, until he was in up to his waist, wading through a slurry of brown mud and murky water. Snakes swam through the water, and overhead, black crows sat in the dead branches of trees, watching him with dark, shiny eyes. When he passed they would scream deep in their throats and wing out over the trees, headed into the center of the swamp.

Just as it was getting dark, Cornstalk arrived at the rounded bark-covered hut of the old wizard. It sat on a mossy hummock that rose up above the water like a tiny island. Blackish-purple smoke curled from the smoke hole. Gathering his courage, Cornstalk drew his war club from his belt and shouldered his way past the bearskin that hung across the doorway.

It was dark inside, and it took a few moments for the young man's eyes to adjust to the lack of light. A small fire sputtered in a cluster of rocks in the center of the lodge, throwing crazy shadows on the bark walls, and Cornstalk's nostrils were stung by the sharp smell of strong herbs.

Then he began to make out shapes—dark forms moving around. He realized that these were the women slaves Waterwoman had mentioned. There were four of them, ragged and dirty, pacing about like captive animals.

One of them knelt by the fire, roasting some bear ribs on the coals. When she looked up, Cornstalk drew in a sharp breath. It was Waterwoman. He hardly recognized her. Her hair was cut short, close to her head. Her skin was smeared with soot and grease and her dress was in tatters. He noticed that she was tied like a dog: a throat cord was wound around her neck and fastened to a large wooden stake driven into the ground nearby.

As Cornstalk was peering around the smoky lodge, a

droplet of fat trickled off the bear ribs, into the fire. The flames flared up.

And Cornstalk could see the evil sorcerer, Old One Eye, sitting against the wall. His shaved head glistened in the firelight and his naked body was covered with horrible blue tattoos.

The old man smiled, his right eye squinted shut, his skin greasy and blue in the firelight. Cornstalk found himself unable to move. The power of that one eye held him in his place.

"Waterwoman!" the old man shouted. "We have a visitor. Make him something to eat!"

Trembling with fear, Waterwoman obeyed. She broke some bear ribs, put them into a wooden bowl, and gave them to Old One Eye. The old man handed the bowl out across the fire.

"Come. Sit and eat with me," the old wizard crooned, his eye drawing Cornstalk toward the fire.

Despite his revulsion, Cornstalk found himself walking across the lodge and reaching for the bowl of meat. Just as his hand was closing around the bowl, Old One Eye snatched it away. The hut filled with the old man's cruel laughter.

"You think I'm going to give this to you?" he taunted. "No, this is food for my fierce hairless bear."

The old man turned and shouted into the darkness, "Ya-Kwa-Hey! Come out here. I have something for you!"

Overcome with fear, Cornstalk watched as a huge bear, naked except for a ridge of hair down its back,

[35]

ambled into the firelight and stood on its hind legs. Its head brushed the tall bark ceiling. Its hot breath warmed the room. Its claws were long and red in the firelight.

Old One Eye rose and handed the bowl of bear ribs up to the monster, who swallowed them in one gulp. Then Old One Eye laughed and pointed at Cornstalk.

With a terrible roar, the Ya-Kwa-Hey lashed out with his paw and struck Cornstalk on the side of the head, knocking him to the ground. Waterwoman wept quietly as the bear sank his teeth into Cornstalk's shoulder and dragged him outside. Then the Ya-Kwa-Hey dragged Cornstalk around to the back of the lodge, where he threw him into a pile of reddened sumac branches. Later, when the Ya-Kwa-Hey was hungry, he would make a meal of the young warrior.

The next morning, when the three brothers awoke and saw that Cornstalk had not returned, Skullplayer did as he had been told. He lifted the flute to his lips and blew a sad, haunting tune. As the brothers watched in horror, a single droplet of red blood trickled out the end of the flute and splashed onto the leaves.

Without a word, Blue Hawk knelt by the fire and began to blacken his face for war.

Slow Turtle and Skullplayer tried to argue with him, reminding him that Cornstalk would not want him to risk his life needlessly. But Blue Hawk's mind was made up. He collected his weapons and set out for the deep of the swamp. All day Skullplayer and Slow Turtle waited.

All day they glanced in the direction of Old One Eye's trail, hoping to see their brothers returning with Waterwoman, safe and sound. But the day passed, and when darkness fell, the young men realized that another brother had fallen prey to the old wizard's magic.

The next morning, when Blue Hawk hadn't returned, Skullplayer played the flute. They saw exactly what they expected: another droplet of blood. Slow Turtle insisted that he must go, and though Skullplayer tried to talk him out of it, his brother was firm. Before he left the camp, Slow Turtle said, "I will die before I let this evil magician defeat us."

The next morning, when Skullplayer woke, he saw that his brother had not returned. Again he blew the sad tune. Again another droplet of blood fell from the end of the flute.

Now Skullplayer was alone. He knew his brothers were dead and that Waterwoman was still a captive somewhere back in the swamp. He also knew that none of this would have happened if he had been more vigilant, if he had done as he had been told.

Now there was only one way to erase that shame. Skullplayer knew what he must do. He knelt by the fire and blackened his face for war. But what weapons would he take? He had never had any interest in war clubs or bows and arrows. Then he remembered his bobcat skull. It suddenly became clear to him that as long as he had his throwing skull, he would be well-armed.

Settling the skull into his buckskin shoulder bag,

Skullplayer tucked his brother's love flute into his belt and set off for the camp of the evil wizard.

Following the trail of broken branches, he soon came to a path that ran along a creek. In this moist place he saw a toad sitting in the center of the trail. Skullplayer picked him up and examined him. Then to his astonishment the toad made a sound.

"We will killem," he thrumped. "We will killem. We will killem."

Skullplayer suddenly understood that the toad was offering his help. Gratefully Skullplayer dropped the toad into the mouth of his bag and walked on. In a few more steps he noticed a blacksnake crawling down the trail toward him. The snake stopped and lay in the center of the trail. From inside the bag the boy heard the muffled thrumping of the toad. "We will killem. We will killem."

He knew then that the snake had also come to help him. He knelt down and held the mouth of his shoulder bag open. The snake crawled into the bag, curling up beside the bobcat skull and the toad.

In a few more steps an otter came bounding down the trail. He stood before the boy, holding his front paws together. Skullplayer understood: the otter meant to hang around his neck, disguising himself as an otter-skin tobacco pouch. The boy lifted the sleek animal up and hung him on his chest.

The last animal to come out of the woods was

a weasel, quick-footed, sharp-toothed, and sly. Skullplayer held open his bag and the weasel leaped inside.

With that bagful of animals, Skullplayer felt his courage renewed. He walked all that day, and at last, late in the afternoon, he found his way to the bark-covered lodge of Old One Eye. When he saw the strange black-ish-purple smoke that belched from the smoke hole, he became afraid. But he knew what he had to do.

He pushed aside the bearskin across the doorway and stepped inside. Instantly he was struck by the sharp smell of the herbs. In the light that fell through the smoke hole, Skullplayer could see four women slaves moving about, tethered by throat cords. One of them he recognized as Waterwoman. The others were younger, one nothing more than a girl almost his age.

A voice from the back of the lodge shouted, "Waterwoman! We have another visitor. How fortunate we've been these last few days! Cook him something to eat!"

Skullplayer watched as Waterwoman knelt by the fire, broke some bear ribs, put them into a bowl, and handed them to Old One Eye.

For an instant Waterwoman caught Skullplayer's eye. She shifted her eyes over to the bowl in the old man's hand, then shook her head. The boy understood.

Then Waterwoman added some sticks to the fire, fanning the flames so that the boy could see better.

"Yes," the old wizard growled. "Put more wood on the fire. Let him see me as I really am."

When the flames sprang up, Skullplayer was horrified by what he saw. The tattoos of blue snakes and lizards and insects that covered the old man's body seemed to almost come alive in the firelight. The old man laughed, his missing eye squinted shut. He tried to fix his good eye on Skullplayer, but the boy was not looking directly at him.

"Come," the old man said. "Sit beside me and share this meal."

Skullplayer didn't move from his spot by the doorway.

"I didn't come to eat," he said simply.

The old man cast a one-eyed glance around the lodge. "Did you hear that, women? He did not come to eat! Well, if you are not hungry, maybe you will sit by the fire and smoke with me. I see you have a fine tobacco pouch."

Skullplayer nodded. "I will smoke with you."

Chuckling to himself, Old One Eye reached for his clay pipe and began filling it with tobacco.

Skullplayer reached into his bag and pulled out his own pipe. It was made from two animals. The toad, with its mouth held open, formed the bowl of the pipe, and the snake, with its body held stiff, formed the long stem. Skullplayer sprinkled a handful of tobacco into the toad's mouth and put the end of the snake's tail into his own mouth. He lifted a burning branch from the fire and held the flame in front of the toad's lips. The toad sucked the flame in and exhaled puffs of smoke, saying each time, "We will killem. We will killem. We will killem."

"That pipe sounds enchanted!" the wizard exclaimed.

"No," said Skullplayer casually, "that's the natural way for it to sound."

The old man leaned forward and pointed with the stem of his clay pipe.

"I know who you are and I know why you have come. There is nothing you can do to defeat me. Your brothers are dead and these women are my prisoners for as long as I wish to keep them. As for you, I could kill you right now. But I see that you are different from the others. You have a talent for magic. Since your own family is now gone, I will invite you to stay here with me. I will raise you as my own son and teach you the black arts. Someday you will become a powerful wizard like me."

Skullplayer shook his head. "Never."

But before Old One Eye could answer, they were interrupted. The weasel had grown restless inside the bag and had crawled out to perch itself on Skullplayer's shoulder.

Old One Eye smiled. "I see you have a pet. I have a pet too. Why don't we fight our pets against each other—a battle to the death. If your weasel wins, you can take these four women and go in safety from this place."

Skullplayer smiled. "And if my weasel loses?"

Old One Eye smiled back. "Then you must become my slave."

Skullplayer gathered his courage. "Bring on your pet," he said.

Old One Eye laughed. "Ya-Kwa-Hey! I have something for you!"

The huge hairless bear rose from the shadows and lumbered forward on its hind legs. Old One Eye handed the bear ribs up to the bear, and the beast swallowed them in one gulp. Then Old One Eye just pointed at the weasel.

The Ya-Kwa-Hey came walking across that lodge roaring with a roar that shook the ground beneath their feet.

Just then the pipe in Skullplayer's hands came to life. The toad hopped right up to the bear and began belching fire at his legs. The snake slithered up and began striking at the bear's hindquarters. The otter leaped from the boy's neck and sank its sharp teeth into the bear's shoulder. Taken by surprise, the great bear fell backward in pain and began rolling around on the floor of the lodge, trying to shake the animals free. The weasel watched from the safety of Skullplayer's shoulder, fixing its beady eyes on the great beast. Then, while the bear was roaring, his mouth wide open, the weasel leaped off Skullplayer's shoulder and disappeared down the bear's throat!

The Ya-Kwa-Hey thrashed around, groaning in pain and raking with its claws at its chest. Suddenly, with a great groan, the bear fell back and lay still, its mouth open. The weasel came scrambling out past the bear's terrible teeth, leaped through the air, and landed on Skullplayer's shoulder.

Old One Eye looked. There, in the weasel's needle-sharp teeth, was the bear's dripping heart.

Old One Eye stared in disbelief. "You've killed it. You've killed my Ya-Kwa-Hey. Now I must kill you." He reached back into the darkness for his ironwood club.

But before he could touch it, Skullplayer reached into his pouch and pulled out his bobcat skull.

The toad croaked, "We will killem. We will killem. We will killem."

The wizard, his voice quavering in fear, pointed to the polished skull that rested comfortably in the boy's palm.

"What's that?" he asked.

Skullplayer didn't answer. He just threw the skull. It flew through the air, and the sharp bobcat teeth bit and stuck into Old One Eye's forehead. The old man gave a great cry and collapsed onto the ground.

Waterwoman rushed up. "Good work, Skullplayer! You've done what no one else has ever been able to do.

You have struck him down. But he is not dead yet. We need to take the bodies of Old One Eye and the Ya-Kwa-Hey and set them on fire. When they are burned to ashes, they will really be dead."

So they did that. Skullplayer untied the women and gathered his animals. Working together, they piled dried brush around the outer walls of the bark lodge. Using a torch lit from the wizard's fire, Skullplayer set the brush to burning. Soon the entire hut was engulfed in flames, sending up a huge cloud of blackish-purple smoke that blotted out the sky.

Skullplayer turned to Waterwoman. "I'm glad I could help you, but I wish there were something I could have done for my brothers."

"Maybe you still can," she said.

Waterwoman led him around to the place behind the lodge where the limp bodies of his brothers lay in the leaves.

"Listen carefully," she said. "I see you brought the flute. That is good. Stand over your oldest brother's body and play a love tune."

Skullplayer didn't understand, but he did as he was asked. He stood over the spot where his brother lay on his back in the leaves. Overcome with sadness, he blew a mournful tune into the cedar wood. When he finished, a single droplet of blood fell from the flute and landed on Cornstalk's cheek. Instantly the color began to come back into his face. He opened his eyes and sprang up, alive and well, into Waterwoman's arms.

Then Skullplayer played the flute over Blue Hawk's and Slow Turtle's bodies and brought both of them back to life.

As the sun was dipping down, they turned their backs on that evil place and headed home, leaving the burning lodge behind them. They went back to their hunting camp—the four brothers, the four women, and the four animals who had come to help them. And if they haven't died, they may be living there yet.

THE BEAR'S EYELASH

Long ago, a man became so disgusted with his life that he decided to leave his wife and two small children and go off into the wilderness in search of some remedy for the sadness that had overtaken him in his middle years.

He slipped away from his cabin early one morning while his wife and children were asleep, not knowing how long he would be gone or if he would ever return. He took his longbow and his quiver of arrows, and he did what men usually did in those days when they didn't know what else to do: He went bear hunting.

He climbed higher and higher up into the mountains, until he came to the bears' caves, a place where humans never go. Unless they are hunting for bear.

It was fall and the bears were doing their last bit of foraging before their long winter's sleep. The man watched as a huge black bear wandered through the leafless trees looking for food. The man drew an arrow from his quiver. These were special bear-hunting arrows with small, extremely sharp points that would penetrate the bear's thick hide and sink deep into the body, piercing the heart and lungs.

The man sat very quietly, waiting for the bear to come within range. At last the huge beast was less than thirty paces away, downwind, facing to the side, offering the man a clear shot of the heart and lung area. Moving with the utmost care, the man nocked his arrow, drew back the string to his cheek, and sighted in on a single hair on the bear's rib cage. He held his breath and released the arrow.

The man heard a loud grunt as the arrow struck the bear, plunging deep into its side. Without ever looking back, the bear turned and ran uphill into the rocks.

Keenly aware of the danger of following a wounded bear, the man nocked another arrow and moved ahead carefully, following the droplets of blood on the ground. In a short time he came to a rocky cave. Crouching down, he peered inside. And there, in the half-darkness of that cave, was the bear, holding the man's arrow out to him.

Then in a deep, rumbling voice, the bear spoke to the man. "Here is your weapon. You can't harm me."

The man was astonished.

"You were very brave to come here," the bear continued, "but you were also very foolish. I could kill you now for your stupidity. But because you have a brave heart and because there is something you want to know, I will spare you. In fact, I may even be able to teach you something."

"I can see that you are strong and powerful," the man said. "But my life is without strength or power. What can you teach me?"

"If you want to learn something about the strength of a bear, spend the winter with me here in this cave. When spring comes, you will know what it means to be a bear."

Since he had no other place to go, the man agreed. The bear seemed strong and wise and compassionate. He seemed at ease with himself and his surroundings. The man thought that if he could be more like this great bear, maybe he could return to his family and be happy once again. So the man moved into the cave with the bear.

In the fading days of autumn, the bear took the man out each day, showing him the plants and animals that would give him nourishment. He showed the man how to collect dried berries and how to catch fish in a swift-flowing stream.

As winter approached, the man noticed strange changes coming over him. The more time he spent with the bear, the more bearlike he became. Sometimes he would wake in the morning and find himself sniffing at the wind the way a bear sniffs the wind. Sometimes when he rolled over in his sleep at night, he was surprised to hear himself give a low growl. But more than all these things, he noticed that his face and hands were becoming covered with a coarse black fur like a bear's fur. His nails grew long and black.

At last the dark days came and the man surrendered himself to the sleep of a bear. In that deep sleep he dreamed bear dreams and became a bear man, covered in coarse black fur. Months passed as the winter winds howled outside their cave.

In his winter dreams the bear man came to know what it was to be thick-furred, sharp-clawed, and wise. He came to know the special attributes of the Bear Way, and at last he came to understand how the bear fit into the great web of life. All of these things were revealed to him in his bear dreams.

Then one day as the first rains of spring were falling, the dreams ended and the bear man felt himself coming out of the darkness, waking to a new life in a new season. As he opened his eyes, he could hear the deep, rumbling voice of the bear, speaking close to his ear.

"Your time with me will soon be over," the bear said. "The human beings will come here from the village in the valley. They will bring their dogs and their bows, and this year they will kill me."

"No!" the bear man protested. He sat up and shook the swirling clouds of slumber from his head.

The bear nodded. "Do not worry. This is simply the way it is. They will kill me and take off my skin. Then they will pack up my meat to take down to the village. Then they will find you and take you home to your wife and children."

"But what if I am not ready to go back?" the bear man asked.

"You will be ready," the bear assured him. Then the bear gave him specific instructions on what he must do to become human again. The bear man listened carefully.

When the bear finished, a great sadness settled over the bear man.

"But what about you?" he asked. "I will miss your company."

"And I will miss yours. You have been a good man to dream with. But this will not be the end of me. Even though I will be killed, nothing will be lost, provided you do something for me."

"My friend, I would do anything for you."

"Then do this," the bear said. "Go to the spot where I have been killed. Pick up handfuls of leaves and scatter them across my blood on the ground. Make a pile of leaves there. Then as they are leading you away, just before you go down over the edge of the hill, look back. Look back over your right shoulder at that pile of leaves. And you will see something."

The bear man didn't understand that. But as the bear had foretold, the hunters came just as the last of the snow melted.

They woke one morning to the sound of barking dogs. Before the bear man could rise from his sleeping place, he saw his companion spring to his feet and charge to the mouth of the cave to meet the hunters' arrows. In an instant his friend's body was filled with a dozen arrow shafts. The great bear took a single step forward and collapsed onto the ground, dead.

A great shout of joy went up from the small band of hunters. Each hunter solemnly knelt by the head of the great bear and spoke, offering thanks for the food and clothing that would come from the huge carcass. With the dogs yelping and cavorting around the body of the dead bear, the hunters drew their knives and began taking off the bear's skin and butchering his meat, packing it into large bags to carry down to the village.

It was in the midst of this noise and confusion that the bear man came walking out of the cave. He began to remember what it was like to be a hunter, and he wanted to be among them and share their joy.

Everyone, even the dogs, fell silent when the bear man stepped out into the sunlight.

"Look!" shouted one of the hunters. "There's another bear! Shoot him!"

The men reached for their bows. But one man, who seemed to be the leader, stopped them.

"That's not a bear," he said. "Look at him! He has the features of a man. Why, that must be the man who was lost in the mountains last fall. We'll take him home to his wife. She'll be glad to see him."

The leader of the hunting party walked up to the bear man.

"Are you a human or a bear?" he asked.

The bear man was suddenly conscious of how he must look, covered in hair.

"I am halfway between," he answered, "but with your help, I can shed this hair and become a man again."

The leader smiled. "You needn't be afraid of us. We will do what we can to help you. All we will ask is that you tell us the story of your adventure."

The bear man said that he would, and the hunters, with many a curious glance in his direction, went back to the work of skinning and butchering.

For a long time the bear man watched them break his friend's body down into pieces and prepare it for carrying. He thought of the many times he himself had hunted, skinned, and butchered wild animals. He remembered the deep satisfaction that a hunter has when he knows that he has given his family the nourishment they need.

But on the heels of such a feeling, a deep sadness settled over him. Because he knew that, just as the bear had said, "This is simply the way it is." He knew that to live, men must hunt and kill.

While the hunters were engrossed in their work, the bear man walked over to the mouth of the cave, where the bear had been killed. He bent down and picked up handfuls of leaves, scattering them out across his friend's blood, making a pile of leaves there.

Then when the hunters had loaded the meat onto

their backs, the bear man followed them down the mountainside. But just before he went down over the edge of the hill, he looked back over his right shoulder at the pile of leaves.

As soon as he did, he saw a huge bear rise up out of the leaves, shake himself, and go off into the woods. The bear man smiled. He knew that by some strange magic his friend had come back to life.

The bear man told his story to the hunters as they were walking down to the village. He ended by saying, "Whatever you do, don't let my wife and children see me this way, covered with coarse black hair. Take me and lock me up in an empty house on the edge of the village. Let me sleep there for four days and four nights. And when I wake, I'll be a man again. I won't be a bear man anymore."

True to their word, the hunters did that. They locked him up in an abandoned cabin outside the village and guarded the door so that no one would disturb his slumbering.

But you know how human beings are. One of the hunters just couldn't resist going home and telling his wife about the strange man they had found in the woods. His wife told their children, their children told their friends, and before long everyone 'in the village knew exactly what had happened. The news soon reached the bear man's family.

His wife and children rushed to the cabin on the edge of the village.

The leader sat with his back against the door and watched their approach. The other hunters shrank from his glance. He knew that keeping a secret among humans is hard.

The bear man's wife walked up to the leader and nodded.

"I've come to see my husband," she said simply. "And I have brought his children. He has been missing now for months. Great was our joy and surprise when we heard that he was alive and well."

The leader said, "He is alive. But not well. Right now he looks more like a bear than a man. You must understand that it will take him some time to become fully human again. Go home and come back later. I will send word when it is time."

But the bear man's wife and children did not understand. They had missed the man so deeply and worried about him so often that their desire to see him, here and now, was overpowering.

But the leader refused to change his mind. He posted the hunters as guards at the cabin door and he himself slept by the abandoned house each night.

The bear man's wife and children spent the next four days crying outside the door, begging the leader to allow them inside, if only for a moment, so they could catch a glimpse of the man who had been missing for so long.

Finally, on the fourth night, the hunter who had betrayed the bear man's secret grew weary of the family's cries and hissed, "Enough! I am sick of it!"

He looked around. It was very late. Only he, the woman, and the two children were awake. The leader and the other three hunters were sleeping under some trees nearby.

"If you will stop this pitiful crying I will let you inside, but only for a moment. You must be very quiet, and you must not tell anyone what I have done."

The family agreed. With a glance toward the sleeping men, the hunter unbolted the door and watched as the woman and her children slipped inside. The woman carried a small candle for light. She held it high and shone it around the room until her eyes fell on the bear man. He lay asleep on a pile of leaves, his body still covered in hair. But his children didn't mind when they saw him. They took him by his hairy arms and helped him to his feet. He was groggy, but he moved with the strength of a bear. The hunter who had opened the door for them became afraid and fell back, letting them pass.

Under cover of darkness, they walked the bear man right down the main road through the village, took him into their cabin, and covered him with blankets. The next morning his wife made him cornmeal pudding.

But he wouldn't eat it. The bear man spoke to his wife and children in a gruff voice.

"I can't breathe in this house," he told them. "I must be out in the open air."

He insisted on sleeping in a pile of leaves up against the southern wall of the house. And though he was often hungry, he refused his wife's food. Instead, he went rummaging through the forest looking for rotten logs full of grubs, as a bear will. This became quite embarrassing for the family, and it wasn't long before the village gossips starting saying bad things about them.

Soon the bear man's wife became so disgusted that she did what women usually did in those days when they didn't know what else to do: She went to the old witchy-woman who lived out in the woods.

As the wife made her way past the cabins, she felt as if the eyes of the entire village were upon her, watching from windows and from behind fences. They knew where she was going. People began to whisper even as she passed.

In times of trouble, the man's wife had called on the old woman before. It was the witchy-woman's wrinkled hands that had delivered their son and daughter safely into the world. It was her herbs and potions that had eased the pain of childbirth and injuries. And many times the man's wife had heard of people who had been cured of sickness or healed from dangerous wounds by the witchy-one's magic. But what could the old woman do about a husband who had become like a bear?

Coming into the forest on the edge of the village, the bear man's wife saw a wisp of smoke drifting from the clearing where the old hag's house stood. A moment later she could see that it came from an open fire built on the ground outside the witch's door. The old woman was there, muttering and humming to herself as she stirred and sprinkled herbs into an iron pot suspended over the crackling fire by a long black chain attached to a tree branch overhead. The old woman herself was small, almost frail, with a long shock of thatchy white hair that cascaded down her black dress, almost touching the ground.

The young woman walked up to her, stopping at a respectful distance. Then she spoke.

"Old woman," she said. "Will you help me?"

The witchy-one never looked up from her cauldron. She just continued stirring and sprinkling. The potion began to boil, steam vapors rising from the pot.

"Yessss," the old woman said in a voice that was like the sound of water boiling in an iron pot, "I could help you.

"The village gossips have brought me news of your misfortune. And I've given it a great deal of thought. This potion I make now will solve your problem. But—" And here the old woman paused, stirring her cauldron. "I am missing one small ingredient."

"Just tell me what it is," the younger woman replied eagerly. "I'll do my best to fetch it for you."

At last the old hag looked up. She fixed her sharp black eyes on the woman.

"What I need," she said, "is a single...bear's...eyelash."

The woman was stunned. "A b-b-bear's eyelash? Where am I going to get that?"

The old woman went back to her stirring.

"I don't know," she said casually. "I suppose you'd have to go to a bear."

She would say nothing more.

Puzzled, the bear man's wife turned and walked back to her house in the village. She said to her children, "I don't know if I can do this. But if I can, I will."

As she was speaking, her eyes fell on a rounded loaf of bread she had baked that morning. There it sat, cooling on the window sill. Suddenly she had an inspiration.

"Maybe I can lure a bear with this," she said. And so, wrapping the fragrant loaf of bread in her apron, she said good-bye to her children and set off for the mountains.

She climbed all that day, higher and higher, until she could see the village in the valley below—a cluster of tiny cabins with smoke curling from the chimneys. Soon she found her way into the high country where the bears make their beds in rocky caves. It was late spring now and she knew the bears would be napping in their caves or up and about foraging for food.

Then she noticed one likely-looking spot—a limestone cave with a weathered pile of leaves in front of it. This would be as good a place as any to begin.

She had another inspiration. She took the loaf of bread from her apron and put it on the pile of leaves. Then she ran and climbed a tree thirty paces away. From there she could watch the entrance to the cave without being seen.

Soon she heard a loud groaning sound coming from the darkness inside the cave. A moment later a huge black bear ambled from the cave, his nose lifted to the wind. He had caught the scent of fresh-baked bread.

As she watched from the safety of the tree, the bear took the loaf between his hairy paws and ate every bit of it. Then he lay down and slept, his head resting on the pile of leaves like a pillow.

As the bear slept, the woman slipped down the tree and made her way down the mountainside to her house. Arriving home, she saw her husband asleep on his pile of leaves. The children asked, "Mother, did you get the eyelash?"

"No, my little ones," she said. "Not today. But maybe tomorrow."

The next morning, bright and early, she baked another loaf of bread. While it was still warm, she wrapped it in her apron and hurried up the mountainside to the bear's cave. She put the second loaf of bread on the pile of leaves. But instead of climbing the tree she hid behind an outcropping of rock maybe ten paces from the entrance to the cave. This required great bravery.

She watched the cave carefully, waiting for the smell of the bread to rouse the bear. Just as he had done the day before, he came from his cave, nose alert, showing his long yellow teeth, licking his lips with his long pink tongue. The bear ate every bit of the bread, then lay down on the leaves and went to sleep. While he was snoring loudly, she slipped away and hurried home.

On the third day she did something even braver. She baked another loaf and put it on the pile of leaves. Then she flattened herself against the outside wall of the cave, just a few feet from where the bear would be lying down, and she waited.

The bear rose from his leafy bed and groaned. Then he ambled out into the sunlight. He passed so close to the woman that the bristly hairs of his shoulder brushed her cheek. But he didn't even seem to notice her. His nose led him to that bread.

The woman remained absolutely still as he ate the entire loaf and lay down on the leaves. He shifted his shoulders once or twice, settling into his leaf bed in the drowsy sunlight. Soon the woman could hear the heavy, regular breathing of the sleeping bear.

This was the moment she had been waiting for. Gathering all of her courage, she circled around the huge body of the sleeping bear. Moving carefully across the dried, crackling leaves, she walked right up to the spot where his great and terrible head rested on that leafy pillow.

The leaves rustled under her feet, and for a moment the bear moved in his sleep as if he would come awake. But then he settled down and his breathing became easy and regular once again.

Now the woman stood a mere foot from the bear's head. To be this close to the powerful beast, to see his long hooked claws and his jagged yellow teeth, to smell the pungent odor of his shaggy body, and to feel the hot, sour breath that ebbed and flowed through his long black snout—that was enough to make anyone crazy with fear.

But the woman knew what she must do. Using her thumb and forefinger, she slowly, carefully reached out and grabbed hold of a single long black wiry eyelash on the bear's head.

She was just about to give it a sharp tug—and run for her life—when the bear opened his eyes and looked at her. Taking her breath in sharply, she drew back.

But the bear quieted her fears, sitting on his haunches and speaking in a great and rumbling voice.

"You are very brave," he said admiringly. "Very brave. I know who you are and why you've come. I knew your husband well. Do what you have to do."

Then he closed his eyes and said quietly, "Do it quickly."

Her eyes wide with wonder, the woman reached out, firmly gripped a single lash on the bear's right eyelid, and gave it a sharp tug.

The bear roared in pain. For one terrible moment she thought he would tear her to pieces. But instead he rose to his full height and stood shivering with pain, holding his paws over the smarting eyelid.

"Thank you!" the woman breathed. She ran a few steps down the mountainside. Then she stopped and turned. She spoke to the bear again, asking, "Is there anything I can do to repay you?"

The bear lowered his paws and looked at the woman with large brown eyes.

"I will ask only one thing: Listen to and remember what I am about to say. Because of your great courage, your husband has a chance to become human again. But he will always remember his bear dreams. There may be times, especially in the fall, when he will want to come out into the woods, far from towns and people, to visit again with me and to dream the dreams of the bear. When he feels this, let him go. He will not stay with me for long, and when he returns he will be more human than ever. Remember this, and you and your husband will grow closer as each season passes."

Then the bear turned and with great dignity went off into the woods. The woman watched him go, remembering his words.

She stared down at the bear's eyelash, held tightly between her thumb and forefinger, scarcely able to believe what she had done. Tucking the precious eyelash into her apron pocket, she ran down the mountainside as fast as her legs could carry her.

She ran all the way to the witchy-woman's house. The old woman was there, before the fire, humming and stirring her cauldron. Gasping for breath, the bear man's wife dashed up to the firepit, reached down into her pocket, and drew out the eyelash, holding it carefully between her thumb and forefinger.

"I did it!" she shouted, her breath coming in great gulps. "Old woman! You should have seen it! The bear spoke to me! He actually spoke! And I was so frightened that I can't believe I actually did it!"

The old woman never looked up. She continued

humming and stirring her pot, gazing down into the frothing brew.

At last she held out her hand.

"Give me the eyelash," she said.

Carefully the woman placed the bear's eyelash on the old woman's wrinkled palm.

The witch drew the eyelash close to her face and examined it carefully.

"Ah, yes," she muttered. "This is a good one. This is a very good one."

She leaned out over her cauldron and dropped the eyelash.

But just then a gust of wind came along and blew that eyelash into the fire. With a sharp hissing sound, it instantly burned up!

The young woman couldn't believe her eyes. For a moment she stood stunned, speechless. Then she felt herself overcome with rage. She grabbed the old woman by the shoulders and began shaking her violently, all the while shouting, "You stupid! You stupid, ignorant old woman. Don't you realize I risked my life for that eyelash!"

The old woman threw her head back, showing her toothless gums, and laughed, a wild, hysterical laugh that filled the clearing in the woods.

The young woman was outraged. She threw the witch to the ground and shouted, "How can you laugh at a time like this? Don't you realize what you've done? Don't you realize what that eyelash meant to me?"

The old witchy-woman slowly got to her feet, brushing the leaves from her dress.

"The eyelash is not important," the old woman said. "Now you go home and do to your husband what you did to that bear."

Her head swimming, the bear man's wife turned and headed home. When she arrived at the cabin door, her children were there to greet her. Her husband, as usual, was asleep in his leaves, still covered with coarse black hair.

"Children," the woman said, "I think the time has come to bake some bread."

So they did. Working together, they mixed the dough and set it to rise. Then they kneaded it down, let it rise again, and finally put it into the oven.

The next morning the woman set a loaf of fresh-baked bread near her husband's sleeping place. As she watched from the window, he rose, smelled the bread, ate every bit of it, then lay down and went to sleep again. This was the first of her food that he had eaten in weeks.

On the following morning, encouraged by her success, she put another loaf beside his bed of leaves. Just as he had done the day before, he ate every bit of it, then bedded down and went back to sleep.

On the third morning she set the last loaf beside her husband and waited for him to wake. He smelled the bread, rose, and taking the loaf in both of his hairy hands, he began to eat.

Knowing what she must do, the bear man's wife slowly walked up behind him. She reached out—and this was as hard for her to do as it had been to grab the bear's eyelash—she reached out and put her hand on his shoulder.

In that instant he turned and looked at her. And for the first time in months she found herself looking into the face of the man she knew.

It was almost the same as she had remembered.

Except for one thing. When she looked more closely, she could see that he had a single missing eyelash.

DARK CATRINA

A hundred and fifty years ago, in the days when wild wolves still roamed the Pennsylvania mountains, there lived a young man named Fiddlin' Jack.

Everyone in the Seven Mountains region said that Jack was the best fiddler they had ever heard. At every harvest dance, at every barn raising, auction, wedding, or funeral, you could always find Jack fiddling away.

There was something about his music, something wild and haunting, that people found irresistible. Women in particular fell under the spell of his tunes. And many a young girl had wrapped herself in moonlight and danced all night to the sound of Jack's fiddle.

Folks said the reason his music was so special was that he hadn't learned it in the usual way. It's true Jack's father had been a fiddler and had taught the young boy a half-dozen tunes. But Jack's real musical training began when he started to take his fiddle out into the woods. All the years he was growing up, Jack roamed the valleys and hillsides, at every hour of the day and night, listening and learning. He would sit up on a hillside at dawn or halfway up a hemlock tree during a full-moon night and use his fiddle to imitate the sounds he heard.

In time he could tuck his fiddle under his chin and imitate all the sounds of the woods: the scream of a panther, the drumming of a ruffed grouse, the hoot of an owl, or the buzz of a dragonfly. When you listened to Jack's music, you could hear the sound of a mountain stream gurgling and splashing over big rocks, or the steady drip-drip of icicles melting in a bears' cave in spring. You could hear a cruel winter's wind howling through the trees during an ice storm, or a gentle breeze fanning a meadow of wildflowers on a sultry summer's day.

And because of that, Jack's music was as much a part of the woods as the great trees themselves.

But even with this great talent, Jack still had to work for a living. Because, as everyone knows, you can't make your living by fiddling. So Jack traveled up and down the mountain valleys, working for the farmers as he went, moving on when he became bored or restless.

Jack lived by the seasons. In spring he plowed and planted. In summer he picked blackberries and staghorn sumac. In fall he cut and stacked firewood. And in winter he hunted wolves.

You see, in those days there were wolves aplenty in the Pennsylvania mountains. They ran in large packs. On winter's nights the farmers in the valley could hear the wolves howling under the pale-faced moon, calling the pack together.

Sometimes the wolves would get bold in winter. Driven by hunger, they would venture down into the barnyards. Slipping through fences and under wooden gates, they would run down and devour farm animals— cows, horses, chickens.

Because of the damage to their livestock and because they were afraid for their children, the farmers decided to offer bounties. Anyone who could bring them a wolf scalp would receive a reward of twenty-five dollars.

The payments were made by Silas McKee, the local constable of Coleville. Old Man McKee, or Sheriff McKee, as some people called him, lived with his wife and daughter on a farm along Spring Creek, at the foot of Bald Eagle Mountain.

Jack would bring his wolf scalps down to the farm every day or so, and McKee would pay him the bounty he had earned. It was a large amount of money for a small amount of work, which suited Jack fine. McKee had the scalps tacked up on the inside wall of his barn to show anyone who wanted to look.

Now, Sheriff McKee was very particular about how the scalps should be taken. They must be clean and fresh, scraped of any fat or meat. And they must have both ears attached. So Jack was always careful to skin his wolves in the prescribed way.

There was one other reason Jack liked to visit

McKee's farm. McKee and his old wife had an eighteen-year-old daughter whom the locals called Dark Catrina. She was beautiful in a dark kind of way. The first thing men noticed about her was her hair. It cascaded down her back like a magnificent waterfall, every strand as black as midnight. Her complexion was the color of an apple blossom. Her figure was straight and strong, full of graceful motion.

You would think a girl like that would have plenty of suitors. But she didn't. In fact, the young men in the valley were a little afraid of her. Some people even whispered that she was a witch, with strange powers.

It was her eyes that scared people off. There was something wild and haunting in them, a glance that could make even a brave man feel unsure.

So most men wanted nothing to do with her. Most men, except for Fiddlin' Jack. He was intrigued by Dark Catrina from the first moment he saw her. He could tell right away that she wasn't like the other girls in the valley.

Jack had first seen her at a barn dance held around harvesttime at a place called Draper's Meadows, up along the Black Moshannon Creek.

As usual, Jack was fiddling that night, fiddling with his music and fiddling with the girls. A dozen girls had danced by him, their eyes flashing, their smiles inviting him to make some move in their direction.

But Jack was strangely attracted to the dark-haired

woman who sat with her father along the western wall of the building, watching everything with those black piercing eyes.

During a break in the music, Jack drew one of his friends aside and asked, "Who is that girl over there, the one with the long black hair?"

The man nodded in her direction. "That's Sheriff McKee's only daughter. They call her Dark Catrina."

"But why isn't she dancing with anyone?" Jack asked.

"She won't have anything to do with men," was all the man would say.

Jack smiled.

"We'll see about that," Jack said, half to himself. He tucked his fiddle under his arm and walked over to where the girl and her father sat. Jack walked right up to the sheriff.

"I hear you're payin' for wolf scalps," Jack began.

McKee squinted up at him. "You as good with a rifle as you are with that fiddle?"

Jack smiled. "Better."

The old man nodded. "You bring me the scalps, you'll get the money."

"I don't believe I've met your daughter," Jack said cordially, turning his winning smile upon her.

Catrina looked back at him, a bit of a smile playing at her lips. For a moment Jack was lost in the deep, fathomless blackness of her eyes. For a moment even he, who had so much power over women, was speechless. Then he recovered.

"Would you like to dance the next set?" he asked.

Catrina never shifted her glance.

"I don't dance," she replied simply. There was something about her way of holding herself that made Jack draw back from her. She was different from the other girls. But he was fascinated by her. Jack knew that if he wanted to win her admiration, he would have to do something besides play a few fancy fiddle tunes.

But then Hannah Gilbert, a big giggling milkmaid from down the valley, came over, tugging at his arm.

"Jack," she squealed, "play a reel for us, something hot and fast! Our feet are on fire and ready to dance!"

And Jack allowed himself to be swept away into the dancing crowd. When he looked over after the next set, he saw that Catrina and her father were gone.

Jack made it a point to stop by the McKee place that fall. Yes, the sheriff said, he was still interested in wolf scalps, and yes, Jack was free to hunt the ridge lines around the McKee farm.

Catrina always greeted him cordially when he came down to the farm with his scalps, but she never engaged in idle conversation. What's more, she always had a strange smile playing at the edges of her lips, as if she knew something that Jack didn't.

All through the early part of winter Jack hunted wolves every moonlit night and visited the farm most every day. During the wolfing season, McKee let him sleep out in the barn. Many a night Jack had lain up in the hayloft, shivering in his thin blankets, thinking of the girls he had known. Sometimes he would think about Dark Catrina, sleeping warm in her room at the back of the farmhouse.

Jack was a very successful wolf hunter. He had brought in more wolf scalps than anyone. He had a special technique for hunting those wolves. He would sit up on the mountainside in the moonlight. He always picked a spot on the edge of a clearing, where the moonlight would fall as brightly as possible, giving him light to shoot by. He himself would stay hidden, back in the shadows at the edge of the forest.

Once he had picked a likely spot, Jack would push two forked sticks into the ground. In one, off to his left, he'd place his fiddle and his bow. In the other, off to his right, he'd set his flintlock rifle.

Jack had learned to draw the bow across the strings of his fiddle in a way that imitated the sound of a wolf howling in the night. He would wait until he heard a wolf howl up on the mountainside. Then he would answer with his fiddle. Gradually the howls would come closer as the wolves tried to locate him. And more often than not, he would fiddle a wolf right down into the clearing.

As soon as the animal got within range, Jack would lay down the fiddle and the bow, placing them in the crook of the forked stick on the left. Then he would pick up his flintlock rifle, and with a single well-placed shot, he would collect himself a wolf scalp.

One night late in January, when the hemlock boughs were heavily weighted with snow and the temperature had dropped below the freezing mark, Jack was hunting wolves in one of his usual spots along the mountainside. The moon rose early, giving him light to shoot by. And further up in the hills, the wolves had begun their lonesome yowling. Jack set his loaded rifle in the forked stick to his right. Then he picked up the fiddle and the bow. Tucking the fiddle under his chin, he drew the waxed horsehair bow across the strings, sending a long sliding fiddle howl out through the frosty air.

As the last note trailed off, he heard the quavering howl of a she-wolf up along the ridge line. Other wolves howled on distant ridges. But this one was close, on the mountaintop just above him. Jack answered with his fiddle, drawing her toward him, just as he had done with so many young girls at barn dances and harvest parties. The female answered again, closer this time.

Peering up into the shadowy trees, Jack could hear the sound of the wolf coming down the trail just above the clearing. A moment later she stepped out into the moonlight and stood frozen, listening, sniffing the air, offering Jack an easy shot.

She was a fair-sized she-wolf, with a dark coat and shining eyes. She wasn't as big as a male, of course, but still big enough for a bounty. In his mind Jack was already counting out the twenty-five dollars her scalp would bring him.

Moving quietly, just as he'd done so many times before, Jack laid down the fiddle and bow and picked up his flintlock rifle. Sighting in on the she-wolf's chest, he held his breath and squeezed the trigger.

The hammer snapped forward, making a sharp metallic click that sounded loud in the quiet of the clearing.

The wolf's ears pricked up. She lifted her nose to the wind and began scanning the edge of the clearing where Jack was hidden.

This was not the first time Jack's gun had misfired. Even the best flintlock rifles did this every now and then. Many things could have caused the problem—wet powder, a dull flint, or a bent flash pan. But whatever the reason, the gun had refused to fire. When this had happened before, the wolf would catch Jack's scent, then turn and retreat into the woods.

But this she-wolf didn't do that. Instead, she put her head down and came straight for Jack, baring her sharp teeth.

Jack drew a large butcher knife from his belt. As she leaped through the air, her jaws reaching for his throat, he lashed out with the knife and managed to cut her across the right front paw. The she-wolf twisted in midair, yelping in pain. She hit the ground running and disappeared into the woods.

Fiddlin' Jack lay in the snow gasping for breath, clutching his knife and listening. If she was coming back, he wanted to be ready for her. But there was no sound, nothing but the wind in the trees and the rasp of his own frightened breathing. She was gone.

Jack had killed many wolves—had even missed a few—but this was the first one that had come for him. A strange fear rose in the young man as he gathered up his fiddle and rifle and made his way down the mountainside to McKee's farm. This was enough wolfing for one night.

Jack rose the next morning, still shaken from his close brush with death. He decided to walk over to the farmhouse and ask for a cup of coffee to quiet his nerves.

Dark Catrina answered the door, her dark eyes sparkling, a smile playing at her lips.

"I just wanted a cup of coff—" Jack began. But then he saw it. Around her right hand was a white cloth bandage, freshly stained with blood.

"Catrina," Jack said in a surprised voice. "Wh-what happened to your hand?"

"Oh," she said coyly, "it's really nothing. It's my own fault. I was careless last night with my mother's butcher knife!"

Jack's scalp suddenly felt hot and prickly. A strange shiver went through him.

Catrina laughed, her dark eyes flashing. "Come in, come in. You must be cold. I was just about to make some coffee."

Jack sat in the kitchen and watched as she measured out the ground coffee and put a kettle of water on the wood stove. But Jack couldn't take his eyes off that bandaged hand.

Just then Old Man McKee came in, thumbing his suspenders up over his shoulders. He looked at Fiddlin' Jack.

"Well," he growled through his scruffy beard, "did you bring me any scalps?"

"Naw," Jack said. "Missed one last night."

Then he looked at Catrina. "But I'll get her tonight," he said.

Catrina smiled and handed Jack a steaming cup of coffee.

Jack drank the brew slowly. Then he thanked the old man and the beautiful young girl and went out into the cold.

Knowing that his life might well depend on the condition of his weapon, Jack wiped down his rifle and put a fresh flint into the jaws of the striker. He walked up into the woods behind the barn. He poured a spot of priming powder into the flash pan, snapped it shut, and took aim at a snow-covered stump. When he squeezed the trigger, the hammer snapped forward, sparks showering into the pan. With a puff of blue smoke, the priming powder ignited. A moment later an ear-punishing roar filled the woods. The round lead bullet smashed into the stump, scattering chunks of rotted wood across the snow. The rifle had fired perfectly. Tonight, Jack told himself, there would be no mistake.

Then he shouldered his shooting bag and trudged back up the mountainside to the clearing. The wolf tracks were still there: a single set pointed uphill in a long loping stride, the right front paw leaving a tinge of blood on the snow. He had not imagined it. The tracks were there, plain as daylight.

Jack followed the she-wolf's trail the rest of the morning and into the afternoon. He expected the she-wolf to run off and den up in the rocks. But instead her tracks looped around through the trees and headed downhill toward the valley, toward the McKee farm.

Eventually Jack lost the trail. But that didn't matter. It was enough to know that this she-wolf was acting strangely, not like any wolf he had ever encountered before. A strange suspicion was growing in his mind. Late in the afternoon he returned and rolled up in his blankets in the hayloft. He would need his rest. He would be up late that night, hunting wolves.

As the cold moon was rising, Jack rose and dressed, collecting his fiddle, his rifle, and his butcher knife, held in a sheath on a belt worn outside his heavy wool coat. As a backup, Jack took along his flintlock horse pistol, shoved into the outside pocket of his coat.

He settled into his hunting spot just as the wolves began to howl up on the ridge. Jack laid out his wolf-hunting gear—his fiddle and bow in the forked stick to the left, his rifle, loaded, primed, and ready to fire in the fork to the right, and on a log beside him, just in case, his heavy-barreled horse pistol, primed and loaded.

Now Jack was ready to begin. He tucked the fiddle under his chin and began fiddling up the wolves. He started out with a few long, quavering howls, then punctuated it with a series of short yips and yowls. The voice of the wolves sang from his strings out across the cold mountainside to the distant ridge. Soon he saw her coming, the sheen of her coat picked up by the moonlight as she trotted up through the trees. He knew it was that same she-wolf. She was limping a little bit, favoring her right front paw.

The female loped out into the clearing and stood, her dark eyes fixed on the spot where Jack was hidden in the shadows. Jack forced himself to remain calm. Just as he had done so many times, Jack laid down his fiddle and bow, picked up his flintlock rifle, and sighted in on that big she-wolf's chest.

He held his breath and pulled the trigger. The hammer snapped forward. A sharp click. A shower of sparks, a puff of blue smoke, then...nothing.

The wolf put her head down and came straight for Jack. She was coming fast now, taking one, two long leaps. By the third she would be on top of him. Jack dropped his rifle and snatched up his pistol. He slipped in the wet snow and fell onto his back. As the long form of the wolf sailed over him, Jack pointed his pistol and jerked the trigger. A deafening explosion filled the clearing and right behind it, the sharp yelp of the she-wolf. She landed in a heap in the snow.

Jack fumbled with his pistol, trying to reload. She turned and looked at him, her eyes dark and glowing in the night. Despite the cold, sweat broke out on Jack's forehead. His hands were trembling. He dropped the pistol and drew his knife.

For a long moment the wolf and the man glared at each other, their breath forming fast clouds in the cold. Then the she-wolf tried to rise and fell back, her back legs collapsing beneath her. Jack could see the blood glistening on her right hind leg. He had made a poor shot. The ball had just grazed her skin, stunning her but making no real wound.

At last she pulled herself to her feet and ran off, favoring her right side, disappearing into the trees.

Cursing his luck, Jack reloaded his pistol and waited. But she didn't return. She was making tracks now, tracks that he would follow the next day.

The next morning Jack made a point of stopping by the McKee house. He was not entirely surprised when Catrina answered the door, walking with a slight limp. He glanced down. Under the hem of her long dress, wrapped tightly around her right ankle, was a white cloth bandage stained with blood.

"Catrina," Jack asked, trying to keep the fear from his voice, "what happened to your ankle?"

"Oh, this?" She laughed lightly. "It's nothing, really. It's just that last night I was—well, I guess you could say that I was a little careless with my father's horse pistol."

Just then the old man came down the back stairs. "I shouldn't keep the thing loaded," he said gruffly. "I shouldn't have it lying around the house like that. Next time somebody might really get hurt."

Then he looked at Jack. "Well, did you bring me anything to tack on my barn wall?"

"No," Jack admitted. "I missed one last night." Then he looked at Catrina. "But I'll get her tonight."

Catrina only smiled as she handed Jack a cup of coffee. "It's supposed to be extra cold tonight," she said. "If you're planning on hunting wolves, you'd better dress warmly."

"Hunting wolves is what I do best," Jack said.

Catrina's dark eyes danced, but she said nothing, that strange smile playing at her lips.

🐺

ALL THAT DAY, as he followed the wolf tracks from the night before, Jack turned the matter over in his mind. Sure enough, the tracks left the clearing and headed down toward the farmhouse, toward the windows behind the house, near the room where Catrina slept. He had heard the wild talk about Catrina being a witch. He didn't believe in witches himself. The only spell he knew was the one he cast himself with the music of his fiddle. The young girls fell under that spell so easily.

Then a strange thought struck Jack. He had never played his fiddle for Catrina. Slowly he began to build a plan. He would catch Catrina unawares that night and he would see how she danced to his tune. He would fight enchantment with enchantment. If she was a she-witch, he would find out that very night.

As the moon was rising, Jack slipped out of the barn, carrying his fiddle in a cloth sack draped over his shoulder. He shoved his horse pistol into the outside pocket of his coat.

Then Jack did something a man should never do. He crawled around through the bushes behind the farmhouse and peered up into Catrina's bedroom window.

There she was, getting ready for bed. He could see her real well. There was a blazing fire in the fireplace. She was seated at her dressing table, her back toward him, staring into her huge mirror and brushing out her long black hair. Jack had once heard her mother say that Catrina loved to brush it out, a hundred strokes, every night.

Jack watched her for a long time as she stared into that mirror, brushing her hair and humming to herself. When she had finished the hundredth stroke, she put her hairbrush down on the table. Then Catrina reached up, grabbed her hair, and with a sharp tug, yanked it off her head! She dropped it down onto the dressing table beside her.

A second later Jack noticed two wolflike ears straightening up on top of her head!

Using the sharp thumbnail of her right hand,

Catrina made a cut right in the center of her forehead. As Jack watched in horror, she began to unwind her skin round and round, the way you'd peel the skin off an apple.

When Jack looked, reflected back in that mirror he could see—not the face of a beautiful girl but the snarling features of a she-wolf!

Jack gripped the window sill, unable to believe what he was seeing, as she unwound her skin, round and round, all the way down to her feet. Then she stepped out of her skin and dropped it into a woven basket on the floor by her night table.

Catrina went down on all fours and began prowling around the room in her wolf form, her dark coat gleaming in the yellow firelight.

The wolves began howling now up in the hills, calling her to join them.

She leaped onto the sill of the window where Jack was hiding. Jack crouched down in the bushes, flattening himself against the wall of the house.

Then he heard a sound above him. The she-wolf was using her paw to undo the latch on the window sill. A moment later she pushed open the window and leaped out, landing on the snowy ground right beside Jack. But she didn't even notice him. She was headed for the hills, where the wolves were in full howl. She took off in a long loping run, as if she were glad to be freed of her human form, glad that she could run with an easy, tireless gait. In a moment she had loped across the field and disappeared into the trees.

Jack knew there was no point in pursuing her. Instead he decided he would slip into the room and wait for her in comfort. He would shoot the wolf-one with his horse pistol as she came scrambling through the window later that night. Then, Jack reasoned, this beautiful girl would be free of the wild wolf spirit that made her so troublesome. Then she would be ready to listen to the sound of Jack's fiddle. And Old Man McKee would be grateful to Jack for freeing his only daughter from enchantment.

With these thoughts in mind, Jack grabbed his fiddle and climbed through the open window into Dark Catrina's room.

It was good to be near the fire after standing in the cold for so long. Jack took off his heavy woolen coat and threw it onto Catrina's bed along with his pistol and his fiddle.

Then Jack's eyes fell on the woven basket. He chuckled to himself.

He picked it up and carried it over to the fireplace. Holding it up to the firelight, he looked inside. Looking up at him from the bottom of the basket was the beautiful face of the girl he knew. Her entire body lay coiled in the woven container, like a coil of rope.

For a second he considered dropping the basket into the flames, thinking about how the skin would sizzle.

That would be one way to get rid of this troublesome problem. But then he would never know what it would be like to have Catrina to himself.

"No," he said, "it would be a real shame to burn the skin of a woman as beautiful as Dark Catrina. I think I'll keep her skin with me."

Jack had known many beautiful women in his time, and he had never known one who could refuse his fiddle. Why should Catrina's skin be different?

It was worth a try. The she-wolf wouldn't be returning for hours, and besides, what better way to pass the time than to play some dancing music for a beautiful girl?

Jack dumped Catrina's skin out on the wooden floor by the hearth. He drew his fiddle from the bag. Quietly, so as not to waken the girl's parents asleep in their bedroom upstairs, he began to play a lively dancing tune. He had fiddled up wolves, and he had fiddled up girls. But could he fiddle up a woman's skin?

He had no sooner launched into one of his lively dancing reels when the skin began to move, winding round and round as if it were being lifted by a whirlwind. Jack chuckled. The magic was working! He played faster.

The coils of skin spun round and round, whirling at terrific speed. Then, staring into the blur of motion before him, Jack could make out the slim form of Dark Catrina, dancing round and round and round. Jack slowed the fiddle music down. Sure enough, there she was—her skin anyway. Jack stopped playing long enough to go over to her dressing table. He arranged her hair on top of her head and draped her white night robe over her shoulders.

He stood back and looked. It was her, all right—all of her except her eyes. There was nothing in there—the skin was empty inside. That dark look in the eyes, which unnerved Jack and so many other men, was gone now. There was nothing inside but emptiness.

"I think I like her better this way," Jack thought.

Then he launched into a lively tune and started dancing her skin round and round. Soon the skin was whirling and dancing, obeying his every command.

Jack laughed. "I like it like this," he said to himself.

Then suddenly Jack felt something cold and icy on the back of his neck. He stopped playing. The skin stopped dancing and stood quietly by the fire.

Jack turned and noticed that the window was still open.

Jack grunted to himself. "A man doesn't want a cold breeze blowing on the back of his neck on a night like this."

But when he stepped over to close the window, he saw something peering in out of the darkness—a pair of shining, wolflike eyes. He backed up, clutching his fiddle.

A moment later the she-wolf dropped down into that window and walked slowly across the wooden floor between Catrina's skin and Jack. The wolf leaped onto the skin, rolled around three times, and when Catrina sat up, she had her eyes back in her!

Now Catrina was moving on her own, even though the fiddle was silent. Without a word, Catrina walked up to Jack, that strange smile playing on her lips. She took the fiddle and bow from his hands and laid them on her bed beside Jack's coat.

Then she led him over to her dressing table, and she was humming a strange, eerie tune, a reel he himself had charmed women with. And just like the women he had enchanted over the years, Jack had to obey.

She sat him down in her dressing chair. She reached for her hairbrush, and as Jack watched helplessly, she began to brush out his thick black hair. A hundred strokes she brushed it, all the while humming that tune.

When she finished that hundredth stroke, she laid the brush down on the table, and smiling into the mirror at Jack, she twined her fingers into his hair. With a sharp motion not unlike the one he used to scalp a wolf, she yanked the hair up off his head and dropped it down on the table before him.

When Jack looked into the mirror, he was astonished to see two wolf ears straightening up on either side of his head.

Then Catrina reached over his shoulder, and using her sharp thumbnail, she made a cut in the center of his forehead and began to unwind his skin round and round. When Jack peered into the mirror he could see a he-wolf underneath him.

She unwound his skin all the way down to his feet and dropped it into a basket. Then she unwound her own skin and dropped it into the basket as well.

A cold wind blew in through the open window, carrying the scent of pine trees and snow. Jack had never smelled anything so intensely before. He sniffed again. Other odors were there—traces of rabbit and elk, limestone and sassafras and dried blackberry bushes. A thrill rippled through his body. He wanted to run now, to feel his four legs beneath him as he raced across the snow.

With a glance in his direction the she-wolf sprang out the window, landing lightly on the ground. In his wolf form Jack leaped. He was easily able to clear the window sill, landing gracefully in the snow beside her. Then they ran, as only wolves can run, with the snowy fields disappearing in fast white sheets beneath them, their eyes teary with cold and excitement as they headed uphill into the trees, onto the ridges where fellow wolves howled.

That night Jack ran with the wolves and became one of them. He came to know the freedom of the moonlight marauders, the excitement of the chase and the kill, the warmth and safety of the rocky brown earth dens on the mountainside. At last, after all those years of hunting wolves, he knew what it was to be one. To run with the pack, graceful and sharp-eyed, looking for food, with miles and miles of moonlit night all to themselves. He and Catrina sat up on the ridge in their wolfy forms, lifting their quavering voices with a dozen other wolves, lost in the lonely joy of howling at the winter's moon.

Jack lived out the rest of his days on the McKee farm. After Sheriff McKee and his wife died, Jack and Catrina raised their own family there. Sometimes at night the whole family would slip out of their skins and go up on the ridge to howl at the moon.

❦

THE LAST OF THE Pennsylvania wolves are gone. Men hunted them down, trapped them, and poisoned them into extinction. And it may be a very long time before these mountains are graced with the lonely music of a wolf's howl. But there is still magic in these hills for anyone who cares to search for it.

Sometimes at night, when the moon is shining just right, some of the local people who live near Bald Eagle Mountain say that if you listen carefully, you can still hear the sound of Jack's fiddle up on the mountainside, fiddling for those wolves.

One old-timer told me that he snuck up there one night, following the fiddle's sound. He looked up through the trees into the clearing where Jack once hunted the wolves.

And there, sitting on a log, was the skin of Fiddlin' Jack, no eyes in the eyeholes, fiddling a strange, eerie tune. And there, in the center of the clearing, was the skin of Dark Catrina, dancing round and round and round.

MOON DOG

Samuel Kittering was a bear hunter by profession. He lived in a cabin way back in the woods, up along the west branch of the Susquehanna River, with his only friend, a big-boned floppy-eared hound dog named Hank. Samuel didn't have much time for people. I guess you could say he was a hermit.

He would always say, "The more time I spend around people, the more I appreciate my dog."

Samuel and Hank had been together six long years. Samuel had gotten him from Zeke Hemsley, a keelboatman who passed up and down the river every now and then on his big thirty-foot wooden boat. Hank was the runt of the litter. Zeke, who had trained many hunting dogs himself, said that Hank would never amount to anything. But from the moment Samuel laid eyes on that pup, he knew he had found himself a good dog.

Samuel was right. Hank turned out to be a natural hunting dog. He had a keen nose and he wasn't afraid to chase a bear into the thicket and keep it at bay until Samuel could get a clear shot with his rifle.

There was only one problem. For some reason Hank was terrified of the water. Even though they lived right along the river, Hank never learned to swim. And whenever they had to cross a stream in the woods, Hank would run back and forth, upstream and downstream, until he found a shallow place to splash across.

But Samuel counted this as a minor flaw. In every other way Hank was the perfect hunting dog. Sam couldn't have picked a better companion for his lonely life in the woods. As the years rolled by, they became very close. They shared the same hardships and the same pleasures and each could hardly imagine life without the other.

They got their living from the woods and streams. In those early days of Pennsylvania, a man who had a good hunting dog and was skillful with a rifle could live for years without any money. For a few essentials, things like gunpowder and lead musket balls, Samuel would barter with the keelboatmen who came downriver, supplying them with fresh meat or deerskins. The truth was, Samuel and Hank needed very little from the outside world.

But Sam had one vice: he liked to smoke a pipe. That meant he needed tobacco. He had tried growing it once or twice in the rocky garden behind the cabin, but he had never had any success. He tried to find a substitute for tobacco in the woods, smoking ground-up willow bark and cedar bark, and once he even tried dried milkweed pods. But these things left him coughing and watery-eyed. He knew what he needed was some real tobacco.

Every now and then a big wooden keelboat would come downriver, carrying a dozen men, every one of them smoking a pipe. Sam would stand on the shore and look longingly out across the water, smelling the fragrance of the tobacco smoke. He would paddle his canoe out and offer to trade a haunch of venison or a wild turkey for a few twists of tobacco. The keelboatmen saw the wild hungering look in his eye and would always take advantage of him, asking for way too much in trade. But Kittering always paid because he loved smoking so much.

His dealings with the keelboatmen confirmed his worst suspicions about the human race. The men always laughed at him because he had no coin money. But eventually Samuel found something to trade that was even more valuable than gold or silver coins. It was Zeke Hemsley who suggested that if Samuel liked smoking tobacco so much, he should start smoking hams as well.

Zeke was right. Kittering soon learned that if there was one thing those keelboatmen couldn't resist, it was a smoked bear ham. Samuel's smoked hams became famous up and down the river, and in time Sam was able to supply all of his tobacco needs by trading his hams.

Of course, before he could smoke the hams, he would have to hunt down the bears, because bears very rarely give up their ham bones willingly. Samuel and

Hank would go up in the woods each fall and hunt every day. In a good year they would kill and dry the meat of a dozen bears.

Sam built a special smokehouse for curing the meat. From the outside it looked like a small shed. The walls and roof of the smokehouse were made of the same sturdy materials as Samuel's cabin: solid hemlock logs hewn square with an axe, chinked with mud and moss, a roof of hickory bark shingles with a small chimney to let out the smoke. The door was made of solid hickory slats with leather hinges and a heavy crossbar to keep intruders out.

Samuel would hang the meat from wooden pegs on the rafters inside the shed. Then he would build a low, smoky fire of hickory and let it burn all night. The smoke would rise up around those hams and dry them out, preserving them for the winter and giving them a smoky, mouth-watering taste that was impossible for any river man to resist.

The smokehouse was built like a tiny fortress because there were thieves in that part of the country. Not human ones—the river men knew better than to mess with a sharpshooter like Sam. There were other thieves in the woods, thieves that enjoyed the hams as much as humans. Cougars, wolves, foxes, even the bears themselves would smell that meat smoking for miles. And many a night Samuel had shot those animals from his front porch as they tried to break into his smoke-house. In the half-dozen years that Samuel had smoked hams, he never lost a single ham to an intruder.

But one year, during the early days of November, a strange thing happened.

Samuel went out to the smokehouse to select a ham for dinner. He and Hank liked smoked hams as much as anyone, so Samuel always made sure that they had enough for both trading and eating.

Samuel pulled open the big hickory-slat door, stepped inside, and took in a deep breath. The savory smoky smell drifted into his nostrils, making his taste buds tingle. But when he reached up for one of the hams, his hand stopped in midair. He squinted into the half-darkness.

"It can't be," he muttered.

One of the hams was missing!

He counted them again just to make sure. They had killed twelve bears that year, which meant twenty-four hams. But there were only twenty-three.

Samuel looked around the smokehouse. He couldn't see any signs of a break-in. There were no tracks or scratch marks. Everything seemed to be in its place except that one missing ham.

Sam walked outside and called Hank.

"Here, boy," he said. "Use that ol' nose of yours. Find out who's been stealin' our ham."

Hank put his nose to the ground and went once, twice around the smokehouse but couldn't pick up any scent. After a few moments he lost interest and went back to his place by the cabin door, where he had been lying in the sun, chewing on an old bear skull.

That night they didn't have ham for dinner—they would have to ration their hams now. So even though they had their appetites set for a meal of smoked bear hams, they settled for roasted squirrel and dried beans.

After dinner, Samuel and Hank sat by the fireplace staring into the flames. Hank fell asleep on the floor by the fire. But Sam couldn't sleep. He just sat there smoking his pipe, staring into the flames, trying to figure out what kind of animal would be clever enough to sneak into the smokehouse and steal a ham without leaving a single sign.

The next morning Samuel woke early, pulled on his boots, and walked out to the smokehouse just to make sure everything was all right. He swung open the door and stepped inside. Looking up, he was astonished by what he saw.

Another ham was missing!

Samuel was furious now. He called his dog.

"Hank! Come 'ere, boy! There's somethin' breakin' in here, sniff him out!"

But Hank couldn't find any sign of an animal.

That night Sam sat up and smoked his pipe, glancing out the window every few moments to check the smokehouse. Everything seemed secure. At last the old hunter turned in, rolling himself up in woolen blankets on his bearskin-covered bed in one corner of the cabin.

But he couldn't sleep. He lay awake for a long time, thinking about the thief. Sam noticed that Hank seemed to be having trouble sleeping as well. The hound lay in his usual place on the cabin floor by the hearth fire. But tonight he whined and kicked. Every now and then he would let out a yelp.

Sam got up and knelt beside him, stroking his head.

"What's wrong, boy? Havin' a nightmare?" Sam asked.

But the dog didn't wake. He just lay there, twitching and whining.

Then Samuel remembered something he had learned as a boy, an old Indian trick for figuring out what a dog is dreaming. It was worth a try.

Kittering went over to his shelf and picked up a big red bandanna. He folded it into a long, narrow strip as children do when they play blindfold games. Carefully, so as not to wake the dog, Samuel laid the blindfold over the closed eyes of the sleeping hound. He left it there until the dog stopped shifting around.

Then he lifted the cloth free and settled into his own bunk. Lying on his back, Sam laid the bandanna over his own eyes. Gradually he drifted off to sleep. In his deep sleep Samuel Kittering began to have the dream that had troubled Hank so. It was like this:

Sam felt Hank waking up on the cabin floor, yawning and stretching his legs. The hound glanced over and

Sam saw himself there, lying in his bunk, snoring away with a bandanna over his eyes. Hank stood and listened to his master's regular breathing. When it seemed certain that the old man was soundly asleep, Hank slunk over to the cabin door, pushed it open with his paw, and slipped out.

It was a cool November night with the moon shining down lonely and bright through the pine trees. The moonlight was so strong it could make a dog go crazy. It could make a dog do something he wouldn't normally do. It could make him into a moon dog.

But Hank wasn't thinking about any of that. All he knew was that he had an overpowering urge to sink his teeth into a smoked bear ham. He made straight for the smokehouse. He leaped up on an old stump, and from there it was an easy jump to the roof of the smokehouse.

Crawling along the shingled roof, Hank came up to the shallow stone chimney. He reached down into the smokehouse and plucked one of the hams from its peg on the rafters, drawing it up through the chimney. The trapdoor on the chimney fell easily into place.

With the huge ham in his mouth, Hank leaped down off the roof and went running, wild and crazy, back into the woods. He stopped under a huge hemlock tree and feasted on the food he loved best. When his hunger was satisfied and his belly was bulging, he still hadn't eaten all of the ham. So, just like a dog will do, he dug a hole in the soft ground nearby and buried that ham. Then he loped back to the cabin, slipped inside, lay down on the floor beside the fire, and went to sleep as if nothing unusual had happened.

That was the dream Samuel Kittering had.

The next morning the old hunter opened his eyes, snatched off his blindfold, and sat up in bed. There was Hank, innocently snoring away in his place by the hearth.

Kittering pulled on his boots, strode out to the smokehouse, and swung open the big hickory-slat door.

Sure enough, another ham was missing!

Sam felt his blood begin to boil.

What's more, he noticed that the missing hams were the ones closest to the chimney.

Sam didn't want to believe it. He didn't want to believe that his own dog Hank was responsible for the crime.

Sam walked outside and examined the ground around the smokehouse. There were plenty of Hank's tracks, leading in every direction. But that didn't prove anything.

Then Samuel noticed one set of tracks leading off into the woods. He began following the trail. But he really didn't need to look at the tracks, because every rock and tree was clear, just as in the dream. Soon he was standing under the huge hemlock. Then Sam saw the signs of digging nearby. Kneeling down, Sam dug in the soft ground with his hands and lifted out three half-eaten bear hams.

Now, one thing about Sam: When he got mad, he had a terrible temper. And he sometimes did things that he regretted later. This was one of those times.

Sam ran back to the clearing and stormed into the cabin, shaking the ham bones at Hank.

"You worthless thief!" Sam bellowed. "Just look at this!"

Hank slowly rose to his feet and backed away from Sam, his eyes filled with fear. He had never seen his master in such a rage.

"I trusted you! You were my partner! We shared and shared alike. And now I find this!" Sam threw those half-eaten hams on the floor in front of Hank.

Hank focused his gaze on those forbidden ham bones and rolled his eyes to the side, the way dogs do when they know they have done something wrong.

If Hank could speak he might have made some excuse about the moonlight and the hunger a dog feels when the air is cool and the moon is bright. But all he could do was whimper and fix Sam with those sad eyes, begging for forgiveness.

But Sam wasn't in the mood for consolation.

"I'll teach you to steal from me!" he roared.

As Hank cowered on the floor, Samuel grabbed a length of rope and tied it around the dog's neck. He snatched up one of those heavy ham bones.

"Come with me," Sam ordered. "Come and get what's coming to you!"

He tied Hank to a tree at the edge of the clearing and

began beating the poor dog on the back and hindquarters with the heavy leg bone. Hank wailed pitifully, but Sam just beat him all the harder.

At last the man was exhausted. His fury spent, Sam sat down on a nearby stump and caught his breath.

When he saw the hurt look in Hank's eyes and the bruises beginning to swell under the big dog's fur, Sam suddenly felt ashamed.

"I'm sorry, boy," he said. "I didn't mean to hurt you like I did. I just lost my temper."

Reassured by the soft tone in Sam's voice, Hank crept over and began to lick the hunter's hand. Sam rested his other hand on the dog's big noble head. He looked into Hank's eyes and felt tears starting up in his own.

He thought about all the years they had spent together there in the woods. He thought about the trails they had run and the dangers they had faced. He remembered the countless times Hank had risked himself so that Samuel could get a clear shot at a black bear or a cougar. And he knew, now that his temper was cooling, that he had done the dog a great injustice.

Wiping the tears from his eyes, Sam patted the dog on the head. "I'm real sorry, boy, real sorry. Old Sam just lost control of himself there for a while."

Then his voice turned stern. He reached down and picked up the ham bone.

"But I'll tell you one thing, boy. This was a bad thing to do and you know it. Don't you?"

Hank whined and licked Sam's hand.

"But you're not getting off that easy. Tonight you'll have to be tied up."

That night Sam let Hank sleep in his usual place by the fire but tied his rope to the leg of the bed so the dog would have no way of running off. Satisfied that he had solved the problem, Sam sat up by the fire, enjoying a pipeful of tobacco. Then he pulled off his boots, crawled into bed, and fell asleep.

The next morning Sam awoke to find the rope gnawed through and Hank missing. Sam pulled on his boots and walked outside. It was a cold, windy morning. He whistled for Hank. But the dog didn't come bounding into the clearing as he usually did when Sam called.

Narrowing his eyes, Sam strode over to the smokehouse and threw open the door. There was Hank lying on the ground, asleep. The dirt floor around him was littered with chewed bear hams.

Sam gave the dog a savage kick.

"You traitor!" he shouted.

The dog sprang to his feet, trembling with fear.

Glancing up, Sam noticed that the trapdoor on the chimney had been torn free. Stark November sunlight streamed down through the opening.

"So you came down the chimney, did you?"

A look of disgust crossed the old hunter's face.

"Hank, I'm through with you."

He turned and stalked out of the smokehouse. Hank

trotted after him, but the old man just brushed him aside.

"Keep away from me!" Sam bellowed. "You're no dog of mine."

Just then Samuel caught sight of a boat out on the river. It was Zeke Hemsley's rig, pulled over in an eddy, tied up on a rock. Leaving his rowers on the boat, Zeke was wading in through the shallows, a heavy sack under his arm.

"Hallo!" Zeke hollered out. He splashed up onto the bank and set the sack on the ground. "This is my last run of the season," Hemsley said. "I'll be puttin' the boat up on blocks for the winter and spending the cold months coon hunting at the farm. I brung you some tobacco here. This'll likely keep ya until spring. You just give me a half dozen of those hams of yours and we'll be square."

Kittering shook his head. "I don't have any hams to trade, Zeke."

Zeke squinted one eye. "What are you talking about, Kittering? I know you started the season with two dozen hams. You didn't eat 'em all yourself, did ya?"

Sam turned and pointed at Hank, who was standing on the edge of the clearing. "That thievin' dog broke into my smokehouse and ruint my hams," Sam said.

Zeke clucked his tongue and shook his head.

"Mind if I had a look at him?"

"Go ahead."

Zeke knelt down and called the dog. Hank trotted

up and sat nobly before the river man. Zeke looked into Hank's eyes and ran his hands over his coat. Then he felt the bruises on the dog's hindquarters.

"Say," Hemsley said, "you haven't been beatin' this dog, have you?"

"You're darned right I have," Samuel said. "And I'll beat him again if he ever tries to steal from me."

Zeke looked for a long time into the dog's eyes, and then he stood up, turning to face Kittering.

"What he did wasn't really his fault. He's got that moonstruck look in his eyes. I had it happen to one of my dogs once, years ago. They get out in that moonlight and something strange just takes them over, and they do all kinds of crazy things."

Samuel frowned. "Moon or no moon, that dog had better not steal from me."

The river man stood there for a long moment, looking at Hank.

"I hate to see a dog mistreated," Zeke said at last. "I wouldn't have let you have him if I thought you were goin' to take yer frustrations out on him. Now, I came here to trade for bear hams. But you tell me you don't have any. All right. I'll strike another bargain with you.

"You can have that sack of tobacco over there. It'll last you the whole winter if you don't get greedy and smoke it all up at once. You give me this dog and we'll call it a square trade. You'll have your tobacco, you'll be free of this dog, and I think we'll all be happier, Hank included."

Samuel walked over and picked up the sack. He looked at Hank.

"Get him out of here," Sam said. "I don't want to look at him."

Zeke took off his belt and fastened it to the hank of rope that was still tied around the dog's neck.

Of course, Hank didn't understand what was happening. He tried to follow Sam back toward the cabin, but Zeke held him tightly.

"Come on, boy," Zeke said. "If you stay here, there's nothing but misery left for you from here on out."

But Hank didn't understand any of that. All he knew was that he wanted to be with Sam and this man was holding him back. The big dog struggled, trying to twist free.

Zeke yelled to a few of the men on the keelboat, telling them to come ashore and give him a hand. Three young fellows jumped down into the water and splashed ashore. Hank struggled hard, but the men managed to lift him up and carry him into the water. He yelped and whined when he saw the water around him. Somehow they got him up on the boat. Hemsley tied him to a big iron ring driven into the deck at the prow. Then they picked up their oars and swung the craft out into the current.

Sam was just opening his cabin door, planning to sit down and enjoy a smoke, when he heard a sound out across the water. Sam turned to see Hank, sitting in the prow of the boat, his muzzle to the sky, letting out a long agonizing howl. The sound reverberated through every fiber of Sam's being. He knew what it was to be lonely. And now he had given away his only friend. Suddenly the prospect of spending the winter alone struck Samuel with full force, jolting him to his senses.

He dropped the bag of tobacco and ran down along the riverbank, waving his arms.

"Come back!" he shouted. "I didn't mean it. That's my dog you got there!"

But the men on the keelboat didn't hear him. They were pulling hard on their oars now, straining to maneuver the boat through a stretch of dangerous water. Sam's shouts and Hank's pitiful howls were almost drowned out by the roar of the rapids.

The wooden boat plunged into the trough of a great wave and water washed up over the deck. For an instant the bow of the boat, the straining oarsmen, and the frightened dog disappeared beneath a great wave. Then a moment later the craft lunged free and was carried on into a new set of rapids.

This was too much for Hank. He tore his rope free from the iron ring and plunged into the cold, moiling waters, swimming hard and strong toward shore, toward land and woods and the man he loved.

Samuel ran along the bank waving his arms and shouting.

But Hank had never learned to swim. The current sucked him under and sped him along like a chip of wood. Samuel caught a glimpse of the dog's wild-eyed, terrified expression as he disappeared under the surface of the surging water.

Keeping his eyes on the spot where his dog had gone down, Kittering tore off his heavy coat and boots and dashed into the water. Swimming with the current, Samuel angled his way through the rapids toward the place where he had seen his dog.

In the great rush of water, it was impossible for Sam to see much of anything. But for a moment, up ahead, Sam thought he caught a glimpse of Hank, paddling through the rapids, his noble head held high, his paws working furiously. But the current was simply too strong for dog or man. It swept them both away.

Hemsley's crew found their bodies about an hour later, washed up in a quiet pool of water a mile downstream. The men who carried them out of the water noticed that the dog and the man were hooked together. They could see that Sam had wrapped his wrist around the rope at Hank's neck.

Although the crew grumbled, Hemsley insisted that they carry the man and the dog upstream and bury them, side by side, in the clearing by the cabin.

"They went down together," Zeke said sadly.

❦

OF COURSE, that was many years ago. The cabin, the smokehouse, and even the graves of Hank and Sam have rotted away and become part of the riverbank.

But people say that on nights when the moon is shining just right, you can sometimes see two ghostly figures poking along down the old bear trails, searching for scents and signs. People say that those are the ghosts of Hank and Sam. And they are together again.

HAIRYWOMAN

homas Treaster unslung his flintlock rifle and sat
down on a big rock.

"Well, Tommy," he said to himself, "you've really
gone and done it now. You've gone and gotten yourself
lost."

That morning Thomas and his older brother Joseph
had left their makeshift camp along Bigfoot Creek,
agreeing to hunt in separate directions and meet back at
camp by dark.

"If you get lost," Joseph had joked, "just remember
it's not you that's lost, it's the camp that's lost."

Some joke. Thomas had walked in a southwesterly
direction all morning, following Bigfoot Creek as it
twisted and turned, then forked and forked again. By
noon he still hadn't seen any game, so he decided to
retrace his steps and head back to camp.

This wasn't as easy as it sounded. Somehow the
young man had left the trail. He couldn't always remember which branch of the stream he had taken, and he
found himself following one of the watercourses in the

blind hope that it would lead him back to camp. He walked all afternoon through deep forests and boggy wetlands, into mountain valleys that led him deeper and deeper into unfamiliar terrain.

Just before sundown the streamline he was following simply ran out, disappearing into a boggy meadow. All afternoon he had been clinging to the vain hope that he would luck onto the right trail and find his way back to camp. But now, as the sun dipped down and the forest grew dark, Thomas knew that he would have to spend the night out in the woods.

The thought terrified him. In all of his eighteen years he had never been this far from home and the farm. If Joe were with him, it would be different. Joe was a real woodsman: he always knew what to do. Five years older than Thomas, Joseph had taken many of these hunting trips on his own, going out for eight to ten days. He would return to the farm with deerskins and venison steaks and wild tales about the wonders he had seen in the deep woods.

So naturally Thomas had looked forward to the day when he'd be old enough to go along. At last, after years of being coaxed and cajoled, Joe said Thomas was ready. It was late in November of 1801 when the brothers had left their parents' farm along the Juniata River in central Pennsylvania. They'd paddled their wooden duck boat downstream, finding their way down the tributaries of Bigfoot Creek into the wild mountain valleys that bordered the Tuscarora Mountain Range. This was rugged, isolated country, miles from any farm or wagon road.

At first Thomas had been overjoyed to see the country he had heard so much about. But as they had plunged deeper into the wilderness, the gloom of the great hemlock forest took hold of him and a nameless fear began to grow. He hadn't expected it to be so wild. Especially at night, the tall trees blotted out even the light of the stars, and the woods were filled with strange sounds—the calls of wild animals and the cries of things that traveled and hunted in the night.

Each day they had hunted out from their camp along the creek. Thomas was a pretty good shot. He killed a fat turkey on his first day in the deep woods. He pretended to enjoy himself. But secretly Thomas longed for the trip to end. He wanted to be back on the farm, around buildings and fields, where the sunlight fell full and strong on everything, where you could see things for what they were.

He didn't say a word to Joseph about his feelings. He was ashamed of his fears and did all he could to hide them. Thomas resolved that he would somehow endure this week in the deep wilderness and then he would never set foot in the dark glades again.

And now here he was, sitting alone in the darkening forest, fighting down the choking, panicked feeling that made him want to cry out and run headlong through the woods, shouting his brother's name, begging Joe to find him and take him home.

While he was thinking these thoughts, Thomas

remembered some solid, practical advice his brother had once given him.

"If you ever get lost," Joe had said, "remember: Double for trouble. Build two smoky signal fires, sending up two columns of smoke. Fire off two rifle shots, close together, every half hour or so. Then just sit tight, keep your wits about you, and I'll come and find you."

It was too late for Joe to see the smoke from his fires, but Thomas thought he should fire off a couple of signal shots. Working quickly in the fading light, Thomas reached into his leather shoulder bag and took out his powder horn and bullet bag and set them on a stump nearby. Checking the priming on his rifle, he fired a shot off into the trees. Moving quickly, he reloaded and fired off another shot.

The explosions made his ears ring. Thomas sat still, straining to hear through the darkness, hoping to hear an answering shot somewhere back in the hills. But there was nothing, just the silence of the great gloomy woods.

Thomas resigned himself to spending the night where he was. He gathered a handful of dried twigs, snapping them from a dead tree that lay on its side. He took his flint and steel from the shooting bag and struck up a small fire, feeding the blaze with twigs until it crackled to life. It was cold enough to see his breath now. Thomas added larger branches, and by the light of the dancing fire he heaped up a pile of leaves for a bed.

He took a few strips of dried deer meat from his pouch, warmed them over the fire, and chewed them halfheartedly, glancing nervously around. At last he pulled up the collar of his woolen hunting coat and burrowed into the leaves.

But sleep wouldn't come. He was tormented by his fears. Every few moments Thomas thought he heard something coming toward him out of the woods. Then he thought he saw things moving around just beyond the rim of the firelight. A dozen times he sat up and gripped his rifle, taking small comfort in knowing he was armed. In this way he worried and shivered through the night. Nothing in the woods came for him. The forest just crowded in close around him, settling on him like a thick blanket of fear, terrifying him in a thousand small ways.

At last the cold dawn came. Thomas blew on the vestiges of the fire and rekindled the blaze. He stood up and stretched his cold-stiffened joints. Then he saw something that he hadn't seen in the fading light the night before. There, impressed in the mud, was a bootprint. Hope flooded through him when he recognized his own track! He could find his way back to camp! All he needed to do was follow the prints.

Scattering the ashes of his fire, Thomas slung his shooting bag over his shoulder, snatched up his rifle, and headed in the direction that the prints were pointed. As he pushed his way through the forest, Thomas was already rehearsing what he would say to Joe when he walked into camp. He wouldn't let his brother know how terrified he had been. He would act as if it had all been a grand adventure.

Maybe he would say, "I was just enjoying myself so much, I decided to spend the night out there." Or he would say, "I just needed to be alone for a while. Nothing like the solitude of the woods to give a fella peace of mind." Then he would add, "You weren't worried about me, were you?"

The truth was, Joe was very worried. When Thomas hadn't returned the night before, Joe had fired off his rifle and shouted his lungs out, searching the dark paths upstream and downstream. But in the dark he couldn't follow his brother's trail. At last Joe returned to camp, resolved to set out at first light and find his younger brother.

If Thomas had followed his brother's advice and stayed where he was, building signal fires and firing off an occasional shot, Joe probably would have found him.

But Thomas didn't do that. Instead he did what lost people usually do. He walked off in the wrong direction, convinced that the place he was looking for was "just over there."

Thomas didn't realize that he was following tracks he had made the night before, wandering aimlessly through the forest. He didn't realize that the direction he had chosen to travel was taking him away from his brother and their camp, sending him deeper and deeper into the wilderness.

A lost person tends to walk fast, driven by fear. And Thomas was no exception. Thomas walked all that day, covering mile after wilderness mile, certain that the place he was searching for was just around the next bend of the creek or just over the next hill. By sundown he was a good twenty miles west of where he should have been.

Darkness found him along a stream deep in the woods, bordered by rocky cliff faces. Thomas slumped down against the rock fall, physically exhausted, exasperated with himself, terrified at the prospect of spending another night alone in the open. To make matters worse, when he reached into his pouch for a strip of deer meat, he discovered that he had left his powder horn and bullet bag on the stump back at his last camp! Cursing his luck, he realized that he hadn't even had the presence of mind to reload his rifle after he had fired off the signal shots. Without powder and ball his gun was useless.

How would he signal his brother now? And if he had to spend several days in the woods before Joe found him, how would he get food to live on?

As Thomas's mind raced over these questions, he happened to glance up and notice what appeared to be a cave in the rockface above him. Comforted at the thought of finding shelter for the night, Thomas scrambled up the rocky wall and pulled himself up onto a ledge that was sheltered by a rocky overhang. It was a good-sized cave, with room for a dozen people to sleep. The rocky floor was covered with leaves. From the look of things, animals had made their home there. The leaves were flattened, and bones from a recent meal lay scattered around the mouth of the cave.

Thomas felt secure here. He would build a big fire at the entrance that would keep any wild animals away. He would roll up in the leaves, which would keep him tolerably warm and dry until his brother found him.

He had time before dark to drag in a good supply of firewood and make up a firepit in a circle of rocks at the entrance. Using his flint and steel, he struck up a fire and soon had a cheerful blaze going. He drew the last two strips of meat from his pouch and put them on the coals to roast.

But the exhaustion from his sleepless night and his day-long walk began to overtake him. The warmth of the fire lulled him into sleep. Before he could even finish cooking his meat, he lay down in the leaves and fell into a deep dreamless slumber.

Thomas slept for several hours, senseless to the world around him, until he was startled by a sound back in the woods. He sat up, gripping his useless rifle. There it was again. A sound like the scream of some wild creature. Then he heard another sound. Something was clambering up the rock wall outside the cave.

Thomas threw a dried hemlock branch onto the fire. Flames shot up, throwing an eerie, flickering light around the entrance to the cave. Then he saw her: There in the eerie glow of the firelight stood a huge eight-foot-tall woman. Her body was covered in thick reddish-brown hair, except for the palms of her hands and her face, which seemed almost human. But her eyes flashed in the firelight, and when she opened her mouth to give a low, guttural growl, Thomas could see that her teeth were long and pointed.

Over her shoulders she carried the body of a white-tailed deer. She dropped the carcass of the deer behind her and stepped into the firelight, growling at the man.

Thomas knew it was useless to try fighting this powerful creature. Instead he reached down and snatched a piece of roasted meat off the fire and handed it up to her as a kind of peace offering. He thought this was something she might understand.

What he didn't know was that this hairywoman had lived deep in the woods her whole life. She had never seen a regular human. She had never been near a fire. And she had never tasted cooked meat.

She didn't seem to know what to make of the fire. To get to Thomas she would have to cross through the fire, and she didn't seem to want to do that. Thomas rose and put the roasted meat on a rock on her side of the fire. Then he backed off, making eating motions with his hands.

The creature seemed to understand. Cautiously she picked up the hot meat with one hand. She looked at it and sniffed it. At last she ate it. From her expression, it seemed to Thomas that she liked it; at least she had stopped growling at him. Encouraged by his success, Thomas lifted the other strip of meat out of the fire and laid it on the rock. The hairywoman snatched it up and devoured it, never taking her eyes off the man.

Next she dragged the deer up into the firelight. Communicating with her hands, she motioned to the deer, then to the fire.

Thomas didn't need any more encouragement.

"Well, Tommy," he said to himself, "as long as she's chewing on that deer, maybe she'll forget about eating you."

He drew his knife and skinned out the deer, laying the carcass on the coals and roasting it. The hairywoman watched with cautious, curious eyes.

He cut the roasted portions from the carcass and laid them on the rock, then backed away, making motions for her to eat.

She did eat. She ate as Thomas had never seen any creature eat in his life. Tearing the strips of hot meat from the carcass, the hairywoman devoured the entire deer, cracking the bones with her teeth and drinking the yellowed marrow inside.

Tired as he was, Thomas didn't get any sleep that night. He lay awake, clutching his knife, knowing that it would be small protection against someone so large and powerful. But the hairywoman didn't bother him. She simply bedded down in the leaves on her side of the fire and dozed off with what looked like a satisfied expression on her face.

The next morning the hairywoman took Thomas hunting with her. She just scooped him up and carried him under her arm. Thomas was amazed by her strength. Even burdened by his weight, she was able to move through the forest at an astonishing speed. She took long, gliding strides, splashing across streams, leaping fallen timbers, and climbing over rocky ledges.

At last they came to a meadow at the edge of a small pond. The hairywoman set Thomas down on a stump and swung herself up into the branches of a large tree at the edge of the pond. At that moment Thomas considered making a break for it, running off into the woods on the chance that he might escape. But something told him that this would be foolish.

What he saw a moment later confirmed his suspicions.

A large doe came walking down through the early morning mist, stopping at the pond to drink. The man watched as the deer, unaware of any danger, gradually worked its way along the edge of the pond and under the tree where the hairywoman hid.

As Thomas watched from the safety of the forest, the hairywoman sprang from the tree and landed squarely on the deer's back, closing her powerful arms around the animal's neck. Wild-eyed, the doe kicked and twisted and managed to pull herself free, running in great zigzag leaps off into the bushes. But the hairywoman was too fast for her. The large woman ran the deer down within a dozen yards, scooping the kicking animal into her hairy embrace and breaking the deer's neck with a sharp twist of her powerful hands.

Seeing that, Thomas abandoned all hope of outrunning the hairywoman.

In an hour Thomas had the entire carcass roasting up on a bed of hardwood coals at the mouth of the cave. As they ate, the man mulled over his choices. It had been terrifying to watch how easily she had caught that deer. If a swift deer couldn't outrun her, he knew he had no chance at all. But the thought of escape was becoming less attractive to Thomas.

The weather had turned cold, and a light snow had begun to fall. If he were now on his own in the woods, he would probably freeze or starve before he made it back to his farm. If he stayed with the hairywoman, he could have shelter and food. As long as she was pleased with his cooking, she would have no reason to harm him, Thomas thought. So he decided he would winter there in the cave by the creek. In the spring he would find a way to slip off and make his way back to his old life.

Over time the hairywoman came to trust that the man wouldn't run off. She went hunting every morning and evening. While she was gone, Thomas did the small chores. He collected firewood, kept the cave neat, and cooked whatever she brought in. They subsisted on a steady diet of deer, rabbits, wild turkey, and an occasional porcupine.

It probably would have gone on like that all winter, except for one thing. It got awfully cold in the cave at night. True, they were out of the wind and weather. But the man had no blanket, only his tattered woolen coat and a few deerskins he had cured and a pile of leaves for a mattress. As the coldest nights of the year howled outside the cave, he would sit up shivering by the fire, praying for spring to come.

The hairywoman, on the other hand, never seemed to be bothered by the cold. With her thick coat of hair, she could curl up in the leaves and sleep perfectly comfortably.

In time Thomas came to envy the warmth of her shaggy coat. And every night he began to move his sleeping place closer to the hairywoman. Then one night as he was huddling close to her for warmth, the hairywoman reached out and wrapped him in her arms. For a moment he was frightened, thinking she would kill him as she did the deer she caught. But instead she simply held him close, in a way that seemed almost tender. He did not resist her embrace.

As the winter months passed, Thomas became quite happy with his life. It was a good feeling to see his hairywoman coming home heavily loaded with game.

She never learned his language and he never learned hers. But they managed to communicate in other ways—with gestures and hand signs, with smiles and sighs and laughter.

When spring came, Thomas had pretty much forgotten about going back to the farm. Gradually he began to forget about his life among the humans. The fear he had felt about being out in the woods had vanished, replaced by a deep calm that filled his days.

After all, he had everything he needed right there—food and shelter, the beauty of the woods, the peace and quiet and contentment of cave life, and the companionship of the shaggy-haired woman. And what's more, it soon became clear that the hairywoman was carrying his child.

They hunted and feasted and lazed the summer away. In the fall, just as the weather was turning cold, the hairywoman came back from hunting one day and presented Thomas with a strapping baby boy. She had birthed him out in the woods and carried him up to the cave wrapped in a deerskin.

When Thomas folded back the skin and saw his new son, he gasped. The boy was unusually big, but that was to be expected. There was something else about the baby. Half of his body—the left side of his head, his left arm and chest, his left hip and leg—was just like a regular human baby's body. But the right side was covered with wispy reddish-brown hair.

After Thomas got over the initial shock, the man

came to admire his son's looks. Besides, he reasoned, hair came in useful at times.

The baby never needed to be nursed. He ate red meat right from the beginning. So there was nothing to prevent the hairywoman from going back to hunting.

Now Thomas had a companion during his days at home in the cave. Fed on fresh venison and cold spring water, the baby grew quickly, much faster than any human child.

But such trouble: the boy got into everything, and the man had to put their possessions up high on a wooden shelf inside the cave. He had to build a stone barrier around the fire so the boy wouldn't roll into the coals and burn himself. But these troubles were more than made up for by the fun of having a new son. Thomas sang to him and taught him a few words in the human language.

That was the best winter of Tom's life. Their cave was well stocked with firewood, and the hairywoman never failed to bring in fresh game. At night they sat up by the fire and sang to the cold stars. Each night they slept huddled together in warm deerskins, hairy, full of dreams.

Then one morning the following spring, while Thomas was playing with his son out in the mouth of the cave, he heard a sound down by the creek bed: the crack of a flintlock rifle. Then he heard a voice. It was his brother's! It was Joe, paddling down the winding course of the creek, firing off his rifle and shouting for his lost brother. As if waking from a dream, Thomas recalled his life among the humans.

He ran to the edge of the rockface and waved his arms, shouting, "Joe! I'm up here, boy!"

Thomas watched as Joe pulled the boat up on some rocks and leaped ashore. Leaving his son behind, Thomas scrambled down the hillside to meet his brother.

Joe grabbed Thomas around the shoulders and hugged him. "Thank God in heaven you're alive!" he exclaimed. "Ma has been worried sick about you. Wouldn't rest until I came back and found ya. I been searchin' these streamlines for days. But that don't matter now. The important thing is that you're alive!"

"Sure am." Thomas grinned. "In fact, I been doing pretty well. Come on up and see my cave."

"Forget the cave," Joe said, tugging him by the arm. "Get in the boat and I'll have you home by Sunday dinner."

"But this is my home," Thomas said, bewildered.

Joe grinned. He understood that his brother had been lost for a long time and had probably picked up some peculiar ideas. "Well, all right, then," Joe said, "I'll come up and sit a spell before we shove off. It'll be good to rest my bones after all this upstream paddling."

Thomas led the way to the cave. They scrambled up the rocky hillside and under the rock overhang.

"How did you survive them winters?" Joe asked as they settled themselves by the fire.

"Oh, I did real well," Thomas said cheerfully. "I've

been living in this cave with a great big eight-foot hairy-woman."

"A great big eight-foot what?"

"Oh, I think you'll like her. She's a real good hunter. She'll be home any time now."

Joe shook his head. "Look, Tommy boy, I know this ordeal has been hard on you. Heck, if I'd been stranded up in the woods as long as you have, I'd be seeing things too—"

Just then Joe caught sight of the little half-boy crawling around in the back of the cave. He squinted into the darkness. "What in creation is that?" he asked.

Thomas beamed with pride. "Oh, that's our son. Come 'ere, Half-Boy. Time you met your uncle Joe."

The little boy crawled across the cave floor and Thomas gathered him up into his arms. "Here he is, Joe. Isn't he something?"

Joe ran his eyes over the half-boy. He was speechless for a moment.

Then he said, "Tom, I don't want to hurt your feelings, but that is the ugliest thing I have ever seen. Look, you've been out here too long. It's—why, it's done things to your mind. You don't belong here. You gather your things up and I'll get you away from this terrible place."

Thomas hugged the half-boy more closely. "I couldn't leave my family," he said.

"Are you crazy?" Joe shouted. "What do you want to do? Live in a cave in the woods your whole life?"

Suddenly it dawned on Thomas that his brother was right. He didn't want to spend his life in a cave in the woods. Sooner or later he was going to hunger to be around his own kind.

"Well," Thomas said reluctantly, "I suppose you're right. I suppose I'll have to take the hairywoman and the half-boy back with me."

Joe shook his head. "Tommy, listen to me. An eight-foot hairywoman would never be accepted back on the farm. You just put that notion out of your head."

The man turned the thought over.

"I guess you're right, Joe," Thomas said at last. "The hairywoman will be fine without me. Just give me a minute and I'll pack up my baby."

Joe laughed. "Are you kidding? Surely you're not considering taking that ugly thing with us? He would never be tolerated back in our world!"

Thomas realized that his brother did have a point. The half-boy would never be accepted back on the farm.

Thomas found himself faced with a terrible decision. He should have known that this day would come sooner or later. He should have known that one day he would have to return to his world, leaving his wild family behind.

"All right," Thomas said quietly. "Give me a moment to gather up my belongings."

The man got his coat and his rifle and a few things he had stored on the wooden shelf back in the cave.

Then he walked over to the little half-boy, laughing and rolling around in the leaves by the fire.

He knew the hairywoman would be home soon, and he wanted the boy to be safe until then. So he devised a plan. He wrapped the boy in a deerskin and placed him well away from the fire. Then he weighed down the corners of the deerskin with three palm-sized heavy rocks so the boy couldn't move. He made sure to pin the boy's arms and legs down firmly, leaving just the eyes, nose, and mouth peering up over the deerskin. Thomas looked at the half-boy for a long moment, brushing back the shaggy reddish hair on his small head. The half-boy looked up at him with brown gleaming eyes full of laughter and life, never dreaming that his father was leaving him.

"Good-bye, son," Thomas said quietly.

Then he felt Joe's hand on his shoulder. "Come on, Tom. Let's go. Leave it behind."

Without looking at the boy, Thomas turned and followed his brother down the hillside.

As soon as Thomas walked out of the cave, the half-boy started to cry. You couldn't blame him. He had never been away from his father. Every day of his life he had spent being held and loved by his dad. And he didn't like being confined in that deerskin. He drew in a lungful of air and let out a long wail.

Thomas tried to shut his ears to his son's crying as he and his brother pushed the boat into the water.

[125]

At that moment the hairywoman was striding along a trail on the ridge above the cave, returning home with her kill, when she heard her baby crying. There was something in the half-boy's wail, something sharp and urgent, that made her drop her deer and scramble down the hillside to the cave. When she got there, she found her son crying, her man gone, her man's things gone.

Then she glanced down the hillside and saw Thomas and his brother jumping into their boat and pushing off downstream.

She snatched up the half-boy and ran down toward the creek. She splashed out into the water. Filled with terror, Joe began paddling fast downstream. The current took them, and the boat picked up speed.

"No, hairywoman," Thomas shouted back to her. "You can't come with me. You're too different from me."

She didn't understand the words he was saying. He was speaking a language she had never learned. But she understood what was happening. She knew that her man was leaving.

She dashed in and out of the creek and sprinted down the length of the bank, passing the boat and running on ahead to a shallow place at the bend of the stream.

She waded out into the water and stood on a rock. As the boat came by, the hairywoman held the half-boy out toward the man. It was as if she was trying to say, "If you don't want me, at least take your own son with you."

But the man shook his head.

"No!" he shouted as the boat swept past. "You keep him with you. He can't come with me. He's too different from me."

A moment later the current pulled the boat around the creek bend and out of sight. The woman stood there for a long time, holding her boy in her arms, trying to understand what had just happened. Then she cradled the half-boy in her arms and walked back up to the cave.

On the way back to civilization, Thomas made Joe promise that he would never tell anyone about the hairywoman or the little half-boy. Joe kept his promise.

Of course, Tom's parents were overjoyed to see their son, who had been missing for nearly two long years. They did everything they could to make him a part of the family once again. And for a time Thomas felt glad to be out of the woods and back among civilized people.

But there was a part of him that couldn't forget his old life in the woods. Sometimes at night, when the moon rose up yellow and full over the mountains to the west, he would wonder what the hairywoman and the half-boy were doing. Sometimes he would dream, seeing his son growing to manhood without ever knowing his father. And sometimes he would see the hairywoman weeping by the fire at night after the boy was asleep.

At last he couldn't stand it anymore. It was a chilly spring day when he left the farm. Without telling anyone, he got the boat and slipped away down the Juniata. It took him two weeks to find his way back down Bigfoot Creek and into the wilderness of the western mountain ranges where he had been lost before. But eventually he was able to find his way back to the cave where he'd lived with the hairywoman and the little half-boy.

But when he came scrambling up the hillside to the mouth of the cave, he was shocked to see that they were gone. There was nothing in the cave but a few old deer bones and some charred wood.

Thomas walked up and down the creek bed looking for his family. Eventually he pushed farther west, into even wilder country. He spent a good part of the summer that way, looking for some clue that would lead him back to the hairywoman and the half-boy.

Then one day while he was walking along a stream, he looked down and saw a strange-looking track in the mud. He knew it was his son's footprint. It had to be him. The left track looked to be made by a regular boy's foot. But the right one was made by a foot covered in hair.

Thomas followed those tracks up into the woods. He found a little wisp of reddish-brown hair caught on a thorn. Then just ahead he saw a column of smoke rising from a hilltop. Thomas raced up and peered through the trees.

There was the half-boy sitting before a blazing fire,

roasting a piece of meat on a stick. From where he stood, Thomas could see only the hairy part of his son's face. Then the boy turned his head and the part that looked human came into view.

Thomas walked into the clearing.

When the half-boy saw his father he gave a yip of joy, dropped his meat stick, and leaped into the man's arms, hugging him as if he had never been gone.

Thomas sat on a nearby log and held his son in his lap, feeling hairy again.

Just then he heard the sound of breaking branches behind him. He spun around. There was the hairywoman, coming up the trail with two rabbits slung over her back.

When she saw Thomas, her eyes flashed angrily and for one terrible moment the man thought she was going to tear him to pieces. But he sat up straight, meeting her gaze with his own, holding his son in his arms.

"I came back," he said simply.

The hairywoman dropped the rabbits and walked slowly across the clearing, coming dangerously close to the man. Thomas knew she could tear him apart at any moment. He was just hoping that she would remember the times they had spent together and that she would forgive him for leaving the way he did.

At last, her features softened and she put her huge hairy arms around the man. Tears trickled from her eyes and fell into her shaggy hair. Thomas smiled, locked in her hairy embrace. He was home, back in the wilds, where he belonged.

🦔

SOME PEOPLE SAY the three of them are still running around out there, in the mountains of central Pennsylvania, somewhere way back in the wilderness.

Even nowadays people will sometimes see signs of the hairy ones up in the woods. It doesn't happen very often. But every now and then somebody will be walking along a creek in the woods—it might happen to you sometime. If you ever look down in the mud, where the animals leave their tracks, you might see some strange-looking footprints.

One pair is huge and looks to be covered in hair. One pair is small and has one regular foot, one hairy. And the third set—well, they look like the footprints of an ordinary man. But they're not. They are the footprints of an ordinary man gone wild.

WHERE DO THESE STORIES COME FROM?

Since 1981 I have made my living as a full-time storyteller. The stories in this book are ones I have told hundreds of times, to audiences and to my own kids at home

Because these are stories from my homeland in the Pennsylvania mountains, they speak to me in a special way, encouraging me to listen to what they are saying as they slowly reveal their secrets. Each one takes on a life of its own. For me, this is the most magical thing about being a modern-day storyteller. I am always surprised and astonished at how these old tales continue to evolve, enchanting listeners regardless of their background or ancestry.

If you'd like to try some of this storytelling, my advice would be to go back to your own ethnic, religious, or regional tradition and find the tales that speak to you. Once you have made this important connection, you can begin to collect stories that will stay with you for the rest of your life. Good luck!

For those who are interested in looking deeper, here are the written sources for the stories in this collection:

STUFFED PANTHER
This tale was collected by folklorist Henry Shoemaker in the early 1900s. He got it from an old Civil War veteran and

panther hunter named Henry Rau, who lived near West Mahantango Creek, in Snyder County, Pennsylvania. Shoemaker's account appears in his *Pennsylvania Songs and Legends* (University of Pennsylvania Press, Philadelphia, 1949).

SKULLPLAYER

You can find this story in M. R. Harrington's excellent book *The Indians of New Jersey: Dickon Among the Lenapes,* (Rutgers University Press, New Brunswick, New Jersey, 1963).

THE BEAR'S EYELASH

This is a compilation of two separate stories. The first is one my father, Robert Moore, read to me when I was a boy. It's the story of the Bear Man, and it comes from James Mooney's "Myths of the Cherokee" (American Bureau of Ethnology Report, 1889). Another version of the Bear Man appears in Corydon Bell's *John Rattling-Gourd of Big Cove* (Macmillan, New York, 1955). The second half of the story is an old motif that appears in African stories. Two examples are *The Lion's Whiskers: Tales of High Africa* by Brent K. Ashabranner (Little Brown, Boston, 1959), and *African Village Folktales,* by Edna Mason Kaula (World, New York, 1968).

DARK CATRINA

I have assembled this story from several traditional mountain motifs. Some of these motifs appear in B. A. Botkin's *A Treasury of American Folklore* (Crown, New York, 1944) in his section on "Witch Tales." You can hear the spoken version of this tale on my audiotape, "Awakening the Hidden Storyteller" (Shambhala, Boston, 1991).

MOON DOG

I heard this story from my father when I was a boy. He learned it from the great artist-naturalist Ernest Thompson Seton. You can find it under the title "A Dog Story" in Seton's *Ernest Thompson Seton's America* (Devin-Adair, Greenwich, Connecticut, 1954).

HAIRYWOMAN

I learned this tale from David Hold, a storyteller, musician, and collector of mountain tales from the Great Smoky Mountains of North Carolina. You can hear David's version on his excellent audio recording "Tailybone and Other Strange Stories." It can be ordered from High Windy Audio, P.O. Box 553, Fairview, N.C. 28730.

ROBIN MOORE

grew up in a world filled with stories and storytellers. He has been a full-time professional storyteller since 1981 and has written several historical novels for young people, as well as a how-to storytelling book for parents and children. The stories in this collection are set in the Seven Mountains region of central Pennsylvania, where his family has lived for nearly two hundred years. Robin lives with his wife, Jacqueline, and their children, Jesse and Rachel, in a stone farmhouse in Montgomery County, Pennsylvania.